CHRISTMAS
IN MY HEART

13

FOCUS ON THE FAMILY®

CHRISTMAS IN MY HEART

A TREASURY OF TIMELESS CHRISTMAS STORIES

13

compiled and edited by
JOE L. WHEELER

TYNDALE HOUSE PUBLISHERS, INC., WHEATON, ILLINOIS

Visit Tyndale's exciting Web site at www.tyndale.com and the author's at
www.joewheelerbooks.com

Focus on the Family is a registered trademark of Focus on the Family, Colorado Springs, Colorado
80920.

Christmas in My Heart is a registered trademark of Joe L. Wheeler and may not be used by
anyone else in any form.

Author photo © 2000 by Joel Springer. All rights reserved.

Woodcut illustrations are from the library of Joe L. Wheeler.

Designed by Alyssa Force

Series designed by Jenny Swanson

Published in association with the literary agency of Alive Communications, Inc., 7680 Goddard
Street, Suite 200, Colorado Springs, Colorado 80920.

Scripture quotations are taken from the *Holy Bible,* King James Version.

Library of Congress Cataloging-in-Publication Data

Christmas in my heart / [compiled by] Joe L. Wheeler.
  p. cm.
  ISBN 0-8423-7127-3 (13)
  1. Christmas stories, American.   I. Wheeler, Joe L., date

PS648.C45C447   1992

813'.010833—dc20

Printed in the United States of America

10   09   08   07   06   05   04
9   8   7   6   5   4   3   2   1

DEDICATION

Two editors have shared a vision for what this
Christmas in My Heart series could become.
The first, Penny Estes Wheeler (the editor who gave
birth to the trade paper Currier and Ives series in 1992),
I dedicated *Christmas in My Heart 6* to.

But the second took up the torch where
Penny Estes Wheeler left off, and has shared the
same enthusiasm and vision for a series of story
collections that is unique in American publishing.
She has agreed with me that there must be no letdown:
each new collection must be the best yet!

Thus it gives me great pleasure to dedicate
this thirteenth collection to

JEANNETTE JOHNSON
of
Review and Herald Publishing Association.

CONTENTS

ACKNOWLEDGMENTS

"Christmas Without Christ," (Introduction) by Joseph Leininger Wheeler. Copyright © 2003. Printed by permission of the author.

"A White Christmas," author unknown. If anyone can provide knowledge of authorship and earliest publication of this old story, please send that information to Joe Wheeler (P.O. Box 1246, Conifer, CO 80433).

"Merry Christmas, Mrs. Moring," by Henry Hurt. Reprinted with permission from the December 1995 *Reader's Digest*. Copyright © 1995, by The Reader's Digest Association, Inc.

"The Night the Stars Sang," by Dorothy Canfield Fisher. Reprinted by permission of Vivian S. Hixson and the Canfield Fisher Estate.

"Christmas Without Grandma Kay," by Robin Jones Gunn. Reprinted by permission of the author.

"And You Shall Receive," by Louis Arthur Cunningham. Published in December 1945 *Canadian Home Journal*. Reprinted by permission of the relatives of the late Mrs. Hortense Cunningham.

"Colin's Christmas Candle," by Barbara Raftery. From *Child Life*, copyright © 1956 by Child's Life, Inc. Used by permission of Children's Better Health Institute, Benjamin Franklin Library & Medical Society, Inc., Indianapolis, Indiana.

"The White Shawl," by Esther Chapman Robb. First published in *Christmas: an American Annual of Christmas Literature & Art, Vol. 10*, copyright © 1940, Augsburg Publishing House. Reprinted by permission of Augsburg Fortress.

"The Thin Little Lonely One," by Annie Hamilton Donnell. Published in *Girl's Own*, Vol. 38.

"Jeanette's Christmas List," by Denise A. Boiko. Published by permission of the author.

"Memories of a Golden Night," by Dorothea Allen McKemie. Published in Dec. 23, 1980 *Woman's Day*. If anyone can provide knowledge of where author or author's next of kin can be found, please send to Joe Wheeler (P.O. Box 1246, Conifer, CO 80433).

"Kitten of Bethlehem," by Ruth C. Ikerman. Published in Decem-

❅ ❅ ❅

HEARTY WISHES

Joseph Leininger Wheeler

INTRODUCTION: CHRISTMAS WITHOUT CHRIST

The very premise—that there could ever be a holiday celebrated without any reference to the reason for the holiday—seems ridiculous, like a scene out of Theater of the Absurd. Yet more and more, where Christmas is concerned, this is exactly what is happening.

The first harbingers—though I didn't realize it then—were Christmas cards that carried the secularized message, "Season's Greetings." That was the first solid indication that a movement had begun to eradicate all references to the only thing that makes Christmas Christmas—and that is Christ.

It has been a long time since a store clerk has wished me a "Merry Christmas!" Instead, it's either that cop-out, "Happy Holidays!" or that inane "Have a good one!" making one feel like calling back, "Have a good *what?*"

The secularizing of Christmas music took over nineteen centuries to happen. Specifically, it occurred during what some call the "Golden Era of Christmas Music" (1934–1958), which spawned secular hits such as "Rudolph the Red-Nosed Reindeer" (1939), "White Christmas" (1940), "I'll Be Home for Christmas" (1943), "Have Yourself a Merry Little Christmas" (1944), "The Christmas Song" (1946), and "Here Comes Santa Claus" (1947). There is nothing wrong with such Christmas songs—indeed I love to hear them, even sing them. What's wrong is their supplanting spiritual Christmas music: "Silver Bells" can never speak to the soul like "Silent Night." If you doubt all this, I invite you to turn on cable television's versions of "Sounds of the Season." (Somewhere along the line, most of them quit calling it "Christmas Music.") I'm confident you'll share my consternation at the discovery that fewer and fewer of the pieces aired have any sacred connotations at all, and the interval between sacred numbers widens with every passing year.

And it doesn't stop with just Christmas. Not long ago at a book-signing, a woman who had been enthusiastically thumbing through my books suddenly dropped one on the table as though it had burned her fingers. She looked at me with an expression bordering on horror, and spat out, "I would *never* buy a book that mentions God in it!"—then stalked out. I thought, *I wonder if that hatred of God extends to the money in her purse?* And even that may be a vanishing part of Americana with the words "In God we trust" being expunged from our money.

A phenomenon that is becoming all too common at book-signings is for browsers to ask if I have any Christmas books that don't contain any references to God, Jesus, or religion. If so, they'd seriously consider buying them. In this respect, Europe is even more secular than we are: less than 2 percent of Western Europeans attend church. A U.K. publisher recently informed my agent that British readers would drop like the proverbial hot potato any book that included Christmas stories that were in any way spiritual.

The media has made much of the Ten Commandments monument outside the Alabama Supreme Court building. It has reacted as though the monument's placement outside a public building were an act of bigotry! It carried my thoughts back to the many times I've done research in the main reading room rotunda of the Library of Congress. As I gazed around me I saw reference after reference to God, His wisdom, and His sustaining power. Might not these same virulent forces next attempt to destroy *all* references to God in our other public buildings?

Clearly, America's early statesmen had no trouble differentiating between a people's reliance on God and the separation of powers. The very bedrock of the American judicial system consists of those four simple words, "So help me, God." For almost two centuries, invoking God's presence in public dialogue and debate was almost a given—and the same for civic and public school activities.

Sadly, parallel to the removal of God from the public sector of American life is the increase in yoking the names of the Deity to swear words and obscenities; hence the continuing bluing of American speech—by both male and female, teenager and child. Gutter language is becoming the norm.

As for the media, one wonders if the American people have become so numbed by continual vulgarity, obscenities, and attacks on Christianity that we are no longer capable of being shocked by anything! Every television season the level of acceptable behavior and speech drops to a new low. The same is true for advertising (with the average twenty-year-old having been exposed to over a million commercials, it has become more powerful than home, school, and church combined). Apparently, if the most sublime piece of Christmas music the Christian church knows, Handel's "Hallelujah Chorus," can help sell a commercial product, advertisers are perfectly willing to pervert that sacred treasure.

SO WHERE DO WE GO FROM HERE?

First of all, and perhaps hardest to consider, we must have the guts to restrict media access—or even pull the plug—during at least the first twelve years of a child's life. Thirty years of researching the subject prior to publishing my 1993 book, *Remote Controlled,* convinced me that neither the media nor advertising is reformable. "View at Your Own Risk" ought to flash on the moment the power button is activated. All the studies reveal that the overwhelming majority of media power brokers (including an extremely high percentage of its luminaries) are almost totally secular in outlook, and attend church rarely if at all. This is the key reason why religion—unless it be New Age or Eastern—is so continually trashed or ridiculed by the media.

Ostensibly, this introduction is about Christmas. But in reality Christmas cannot be effectively dealt with without tackling the larger issue: the rest of the year. In other words, reforming the season of Christmas without reforming the rest will accomplish very little.

And it all begins in the home, regardless of whether there are any children there—or even if a person is single. During my three decades of media research one great truth became increasingly clear to me: we become prisoners of what we feed our minds with. The media's imagery is all prefab, thus our minds have had nothing to do with its creation. The more of it that stacks up in our brains, the less likely we are to have original thoughts left. And since precious little of this media-generated imagery is in harmony with Judeo-Christian values, the more of it an individual is exposed to, the more secular and distant from God that viewer becomes. It is that horrifyingly simple.

So it will come to this: We must take control of the avenues to the souls of those in our household (the only one God holds us accountable for), and say, in effect, *God has not entrusted the media with a pulpit in our living room, He has entrusted it to* us. *The responsibility is* **ours**. It will be extremely time-consuming and demanding if we turn off or strongly control the media, for we will have to fill all those wasted hours (forty-plus a week) with something positive, uplifting, and growth-inducing.

But once such a life-changing decision is made, we'll

be ready for suggestions having to do with bringing Christ back into our Christmas celebrations.

In our home, we will begin by expanding our Christmas season to at least thirty-six days (the twenty-four days of the Advent season and the traditional twelve days of Christmas, concluding with Epiphany/Day of the Wise Men on January 6). We will make a crèche or nativity grouping the focal point of our Christmas season rather than the television set. In fact, the TV set will remain off except for spiritually uplifting specials. Each day, at least one Christ-centered Christmas story will be read. Each evening, carols emphasizing Christ's birth in a manger will be sung or played. For at least twenty-four days (some start Thanksgiving night), the Advent candles and calendar will remain central in family activities. Christmas Eve and Day will be joyful. Then, efforts will be made to emphasize and highlight the spiritual dimensions residing in the twelve days of Christmas (especially New Year's, new beginnings and resolutions; and Epiphany, Day of the Wise Men).

The Christmas season should be a never-to-be-forgotten time to interact with family (both immediate and extended) and friends. Our family will attend and participate in sacred concerts, programs, and dramas. Nightly table games will bring a family closeness that no amount of media or electronic games ever could. Most significant of all, perhaps, will be a philosophical shift from a receiving mode to a giving one. Not mere gift reciprocity but sacrificial giving: giving to those incapable of giving back; making gifts, rather than buying them. In the process, our children will learn that true happiness is a by-product of forgetting self and remembering others, just as Christ did when He was on earth.

If we do all this with our families, and *if* we can persuade others to do likewise, what a difference we can make. After all, Christ turned the entire world upside down with only twelve disciples!

ABOUT THIS THIRTEENTH COLLECTION

Some of the most beloved stories in Series history have had Canadian roots. In this respect, no one has worked harder to unearth these very special stories than has Linda Steinke of Warburg, Alberta. In fact, she is also responsible for finding one of the most powerful stories in this collection, Louis Arthur Cunningham's "And You Shall Receive."

The write-in story of the year? Unquestionably, Dorothy Canfield Fisher's "The Night the Stars Sang" (also known as "As Ye Sow"). It has been gradually working its way to the top of its contenders for over ten years now. Second only to it in terms of reader submissions is Henry Hurt's "Merry Christmas, Mrs. Moring."

Two authors are already known to our readers. One has appeared once before: Ruth C. Ikerman in "The Promise of the Doll" (*Christmas in My Heart 1*). As for Annie Hamilton Donnell, this is her fourth appearance: ("Running Away from Christmas" in *Christmas in My Heart 2*; "Rebecca's Only Way," in *Christmas in My Heart 3*; and "The Beloved House," in *Christmas in My Heart 10*).

And what a range of time periods! Henry Hurt, Robin Jones Gunn, and Denise A. Boiko are contemporary writers. Dorothy Allen McKemie, Ruth C.

Ikerman, and Christine Helsby wrote during the last half of the twentieth century. Barbara Raftery, Esther Chapman Robb, and Mary Geisler Phillips wrote during the middle of the twentieth century. Dorothy Canfield Fisher and Louis Arthur Cunningham wrote during the first half of the twentieth century. And Annie Hamilton Donnell wrote during the last part of the nineteenth century and early part of the twentieth.

Each collection, we work hard to make it the best yet. Your responses will tell us if we have succeeded once again.

CODA

I look forward to hearing from you! Please do keep the stories, responses, and suggestions coming—and not just for Christmas stories. I am putting together collections centered around other genres as well. You may reach me by writing to:

Joe L. Wheeler, Ph.D.
c/o Tyndale House Publishers
351 Executive Drive
Carol Stream, IL 60188

May the Lord bless and guide the ministry of these stories in your home.

Author Unknown

A WHITE CHRISTMAS

Clearly the boy was troubled—deeply troubled—about something, but the minister was afraid he'd say the wrong thing to his seat companion. Outside the swiftly moving train great flakes of snow were sifting down.

Finally the boy stammered out his story.

The minister promised he would watch for him since the boy just could not.

❄ ❄ ❄

This old story apparently predates "Tie a Yellow Ribbon Round the Old Oak Tree," and may even have inspired it.

*T*he train was crowded, and the only seat left was beside a young boy who looked to be no more than fifteen years of age. The minister set his handbag down and sat down beside the boy. Desiring to be pleasant, he made some commonplace remark about the fact that everyone was hurrying home for Christmas; but the boy didn't answer—he had been crying. Puzzled, the minister ceased his attempt at conversation and waited for the boy to speak.

Turning away from him, the minister gazed out the opposite window at the snow-covered landscape. It was going to be a white Christmas, all right. Great flakes were coming down, and the window was almost covered. He thought of the long ride ahead of him and wondered how far the boy had to go. *Too bad the boy is in trouble,* he thought to himself. It didn't seem right for a boy to cry on Christmas Eve.

As if sensing the preacher's thoughts, the boy began to wipe his eyes. When he finally looked around, he was trying to act as if nothing were wrong. The minister smiled at him, and he answered with a tremulous grin that wobbled a bit around the edges.

"It surely looks cold out there," the boy volunteered.

Grasping at the chance to talk, the preacher began to tell him of the cold days he had seen during his boyhood, of the trying job of milking two cows in sub-zero weather, and of the pleasure of a roaring fire in the living room at night after the chores were through.

"You know, I sometimes think we can stand almost anything if we have something nice to look forward to. Take me, for instance—I've been traveling for a long time, and I have a good long trip ahead of me yet; but I know that when I do get home, my family will be waiting for me and my little boy will be looking forward to his Christmas presents. It's a great thing—going home for Christmas."

He watched the boy and saw a quiver pass over the sensitive young face as he choked back a sob, and then answered, "It is—sometimes."

Clumsy remark! said the preacher to himself. *Now you've ventured in where you shouldn't. Perhaps the boy has recently lost his mother or father.* Then aloud he said: "Excuse me, son—maybe I said the wrong thing. I don't know about your troubles, and you don't have to tell me—unless you want to; but I'm a preacher, and I might be able to help you with your problem."

The boy looked at the minister for a moment and then said, "I want to tell you—I've *got* to tell someone!"

"All right, then. Let's hear it."

The boy laid his head back and looked out the window as he began. "I guess I don't deserve much Christmas, but I can't help wanting one. I've been away from home four months now. I became discouraged with school and all the chores I had to do. Nothing enjoyable ever seemed to happen in our town. Father has a store, and he farms on the side. Our place is just on the edge of town. We keep cows, too. I got tired of milking them in the winter mornings before daylight, and then coming home from school to feed and water and milk them all over again. All of the older boys were getting jobs.

"One day I ran away from home. I didn't think much about how bad it was, or how I'd get along after I got to where I was going; I just went. I got on a freight train that went through town early in the morning, and by night I was in St. Louis. I had never seen a place so big as that, and I was scared. I had some money with me, but it didn't last long. I suppose grown folk can tell how old a boy is, no matter how big he looks. They told me to go back home—but see, that was the trouble. I felt that my parents would be displeased with me; and even if they weren't, I dreaded to go sneaking back like a whipped dog. I was terribly lonesome—especially at night. I went home with another boy, but it wasn't like my home.

"Finally I wrote Father. I didn't give him any address, but I told him I'd be on this train today. If they wanted me, I'd stop; if they didn't want me, I'd keep on going. I suppose it was a foolish thing to do; but I just couldn't stand it to think of getting a letter from him telling me he didn't want me back, and I didn't want him to come after me. I figured out this way, so that it would be easier on all of us. But now I'm scared!"

The preacher looked at his young companion, and knew that he meant it.

"What are you afraid of, son?" he asked.

"I'm afraid they won't want me."

"But how will you know?"

The boy rubbed his fist on the steamy windowpane until a small portion was clear. It was growing dark now, and the snow was falling fast, but the few houses stood out as if etched against the soft, fuzzy sky.

"Just a little farther," he said in a low voice, and then he hid his eyes. "I can't look," he said desperately. "I can't."

"What is it you're looking for? Some sign to let you know whether they're expecting you?"

"Yes, that's it," came the muffled reply. "I told Father, if he wanted me back, to tie a white rag in the old apple tree in the front yard. It is near the railroad, and we can see it plainly. We're almost there now—but I can't look!"

He was crying now; the minister's eyes were also misty. Leaning over, he put an arm around the boy and patted his shoulder. "That's all right, son; you don't have to look. I'll be your eyes—I'll tell you when I see it."

"But I'm afraid you won't see it," he sobbed. "I'm afraid they won't tie the rag there; I'm afraid they don't want me any more."

Suddenly the hoarse note of the train's whistle broke in upon them, and the boy sat up. "We're almost there!" he cried. "You look and see—I can't."

The train was slowing to a stop as it came around a long curve. The minister strained his eyes to peer through the falling snow. He must not fail. But he need not have worried, for a half-blind man could have seen that tree.

Laughing and crying, the minister pulled the boy up to the window. "Look there!" he said: "The apple tree is all bloomed out!"

And indeed it was, for upon its bare branches hung, not one, but at least fifty white rags which gaily fluttered in the brisk wind—like victory banners of forgiving love.

Henry Hurt

MERRY CHRISTMAS,
MRS. MORING

Mrs. Moring, the school music director, was dying.
Last rites were administered to her. So what would
happen to the "Hallelujah Chorus" from the Messiah
the teenagers were to sing at the Christmas concert?

❄ ❄ ❄

So many readers have written in about this recent
Reader's Digest _story that it is our write-in story of_
the year.

$\mathcal{D}$anny Moring had settled down to watch the eleven o'clock news in the den of his quiet home in Charleston, South Carolina. His children were tucked in bed. His wife, Allyson, who had complained of a bad case of the flu, was asleep at the other end of the house. Her illness was so severe—fever, chills, cramps, vomiting—that she had isolated herself so she would not pass along the bug to the rest of the family.

Suddenly Danny heard an odd scuffling noise in the kitchen. He went to look. There lay Allyson, curled on the floor in a fetal position. She had pulled herself all the way from their bedroom and now reached toward him, her face distorted in pain.

"Danny, help me. I'm dying," she gasped, her teeth chattering. "I really am."

Her husband was stunned. Allyson, 36, had enjoyed wonderful health—excepting recent surgery for a ruptured spinal disc. Only the day before, she, Danny, and their children—Elizabeth, nine, and Robert, one—had returned home from a Thanksgiving-weekend camping trip.

Danny looked down at Allyson; the skin on her fingers and toes was turning purple. He carried her back to their bedroom and called 911. Then he stroked the wet, dark hair plastered to her face and hugged her icy body to him.

"I've never hurt like this," Allyson whimpered. "It's like pins sticking me all over."

Minutes later, when the emergency crew arrived, Allyson's blood pressure was undetectable. She was placed on a gurney and carried from the house. Standing in the doorway as the ambulance sped off into the night, Danny felt weak. Of all people, how could this be happening to Allyson?

Danny phoned his father to come stay with the children, who were sound asleep. In his mind he could see them, snuggled in bed, innocent to the fact that the very heart of their lives had been plucked out and taken away.

"Stick your tongues way out," Allyson Moring had said to her teenage students at choral practice a few days before she fell ill. "Let's do our warm-up." Then Mrs. Moring, as her pupils called her, exuberantly jutted her own tongue out and led the vocalizing. Awful guttural noises, mixed with nervous giggles, resounded through the music room.

"Now we're ready!" Mrs. Moring said, convinced that nasal cavities were opened, voice ranges extended—and, perhaps most important, egos leveled by laughter. Her gaze swept the 50 youthful faces, and she hooked her arms into the air. She gave a crisp flick of her hands, and young voices rose in sweet unison.

With her high spirits and smiling slate-blue eyes, Mrs. Moring had won over the hearts of her charges at Bishop England High School. They loved to watch her drive into the parking lot, her head bobbing energetically as she filled the car with her own rendition of "I Could Have Danced All Night." Even at her most intense moments of conducting, her face was lit by a half-smile.

Since her earliest days, Allyson, oldest of five girls in a family of six children, had loved music. From the age of five, she had taken piano lessons—and later voice lessons. As a teacher, she believed that music could change lives for the better—that it could foster emotional development and enhance all the good aspects of life, the serious as well as the frivolous. She believed, too, that it could soothe those parts of life that are most difficult. In every sense, Allyson Moring was an apostle for the power of music.

For the 1994 Christmas concert Mrs. Moring's group was attempting one of music's most difficult choral pieces, the "Hallelujah Chorus" from Handel's *Messiah*. A challenge even for adults, the selection would be the centerpiece of the concert—*if* the students could get it right. The very first note had to explode from 50 throats in perfect harmony. Then the parts had to follow one another in a cascade of sound—new voices breaking in upon old with exquisite precision.

For 16 long weeks, the boys and girls had practiced after school, perfecting simpler selections and struggling with Handel's masterpiece. During Mrs. Moring's absence for back surgery, Katherine Allen, 17, a senior who had taken a course in directing music, filled in. But Katherine, slight of build with long blonde hair, had found it hard to manage the large group. Convinced she had failed as a conductor, she vowed she would stick to singing and leave directing to others.

Allyson Moring returned to choir practice, the success of her surgery marred only by a staph infection, for which she was given antibiotics. She finished the medication on Thanksgiving Saturday. Within hours, she had taken to bed with what she believed to be the flu.

❋ ❋ ❋

When Danny Moring reached the hospital, the news was brutally bad. Medicine's oldest enemy—massive

systemic infection, also known as sepsis—had laid siege
to his wife's body. She had gone into septic shock, in
which bacteria overwhelm the body's systems, blood
vessels begin to leak, and vital organs start shutting
down. A doctor took Danny aside and suggested he
gather the family. There was little chance that Allyson
would survive the night.

Gripped by this grim diagnosis, Danny rushed home.
There, he sat on the edge of Elizabeth's bed, kissed her
lightly on the forehead, and nudged the little girl from
her sleep.

"Where's Mom?" Elizabeth asked. Her eyes were
beseeching now, confused, and Danny caught the color
in them—the precise slate-blue of Allyson's.

"Mom went to the hospital," Danny said, tears
welling in his eyes.

"Is Mommy going to die?" she said, her voice wavering.

"Lizzie," he said, "she *could* die, but we're going to
ask God to be with us and we're going to pray and pray
like we've never prayed before."

Elizabeth burst into tears as the two of them hugged
each other. They prayed together, Elizabeth's small
voice begging God to make her mother well. Then
Danny tucked her in. With the light now off, Elizabeth cried in her pillow until sleep brought her peace.

❄ ❄ ❄

Back at the hospital, among the doctors watching
over Allyson was her father, pediatrician Allen
Harrell. As her mother and sisters stood around her

bed, Danny and Dr. Harrell each took one of Allyson's hands. The Morings' parish priest, Father Timothy Watters, stood by.

Allyson Moring's eyes opened for a moment. She looked around at her family and at Father Watters. Her father gently said to her, "Allyson, honey, you're very sick. It would give us all strength if Father Watters gave you the last rites." He rubbed her icy hand.

"Am I going to die?" Allyson asked.

"Honey," her father said, gently squeezing her hand, "this is to give us the strength we need to go forward."

Tears welled in Allyson's eyes, and she closed them. Then the priest touched his fingers to the palms of Allyson's hands and to her forehead, anointing her with oil.

Katherine Allen made her way through the bustling corridor as classes changed at Bishop England High School. Suddenly she was face-to-face with Jessica Boulware, a junior from the choral group. Katherine could tell from Jessica's expression that something was terribly wrong.

"It's not true," said Katherine after hearing the news. "There's no way Mrs. Moring could be that sick."

"I'm serious," said Jessica. "She's been given the last rites." Speechless, the girls stared at each other, feeling empty and alone. Would Mrs. Moring really die? What would happen to the Christmas concert?

The next afternoon, the choral group met to talk about Mrs. Moring. The latest medical reports were dire. It would be almost impossible to stage the Christmas concert, only ten days away. But, more important, what could they do—now—for Mrs. Moring?

Jessica Boulware had an idea.

Allison Moring's infection raged on. At first, in her delirium, she had mumbled about the Christmas concert, telling Danny it had to go on. Then she became totally unresponsive, and was kept alive only by a respirator. Her body swelled so horribly with toxic fluids that her eyes disappeared into bloated flesh.

Danny was standing vigil at her bedside when two of Allyson's colleagues from Bishop England, Barbara and John McPherson, came to the intensive-care unit and handed Danny an audiocassette. "From Allyson's students," Barbara said.

Danny inserted the tape into a small player and turned it on. In a sudden burst, the joyful voices of girls and boys singing Christmas carols filled the cubicle.

Staring into Allyson's face, Danny prayed that she could hear these voices that he knew she loved. Then his own heart jumped as he picked up the high, sweet refrain of one of her favorite songs: "Do you hear what I hear? . . . Do you hear what I hear?"

As Danny prayed for God to let Allyson hear, the singers suddenly began the "Hallelujah Chorus." What happened next astounded him. Allyson's eyelids twitched, and he felt a firm squeeze from her hand. Staring into Allyson's face, he thought he saw a tiny half-smile, as thrilling as any smile he had ever seen.

Danny Moring wept with relief and knew that he would play the tape over and over. Then someone touched him on the shoulder. It was Allyson's father. "Danny," Dr. Harrell said gently, "I cannot let you get your hopes up. Allyson can't survive without a miracle."

But there was no miracle. Pneumonia set in a few days later, and the illness grew worse.

❅ ❅ ❅

"The tape made Mrs. Moring smile!" whooped a girl when Katherine came into the music room the next day. That spark of hope ignited the students. "There's no way we can *not* have the concert," said Jessica.

But who would conduct? All eyes were on Katherine. "I'm not capable of it."

But efforts to find a substitute director failed. One night, Katherine and her mother talked until 1 A.M. Over and over, Katherine insisted, "I'm just not a conductor." But she couldn't stop thinking about Mrs. Moring. She remembered the powerful inspiration the teacher brought to their choral group—and the immense satisfaction they felt when she pushed them to their performing limits.

The next morning, Katherine announced to her parents, "I've decided to do it."

❅ ❅ ❅

Practice resumed. As a perfectionist, Katherine wrestled with the pitch, the pacing, the soloists. But the greatest challenge was keeping the singers together for the "Hallelujah Chorus." "I can't get the altos to hold their parts," Katherine told her parents in frustration. "I just don't see how it can all work." Her sleep was ravaged by nightmares of her own failure—something as a top student she had rarely experienced.

The rehearsals were also clouded by bad news from the hospital. At each grim report, someone would break down crying. Katherine was filled with fear.

On December 8, Charleston's magnificent Grace Episcopal Church opened its doors for the Bishop England Christmas concert. Word had spread about the students who were determined to fulfill their teacher's dream. More than 500 people packed the seats and spilled into the foyer.

In another part of the church, Katherine and the chorus went over the difficult parts one last time. Finally, Katherine called for silence. "We are going to pray together for Mrs. Moring," she said. "And then we're going to go out there and make her proud." As she led the group in the Lord's Prayer, Katherine heard sobs. She struggled for composure herself. Then she addressed them for the last time. "We cannot be emotional," she insisted. "It'll ruin the concert. Keep saying 'This is for Mrs. Moring; this is for Mrs. Moring.' It must be the best we've ever done."

In the darkened sanctuary of the Gothic church, the chorus, holding candles and singing "O Holy Night," made its way down the aisles. When the singers reached the front, the lights came up. Katherine could see Mrs. Moring's family in the front rows, their faces shining with the same hope the singers felt.

Steadying herself, she looked out over the crowd and informed them that their director was deathly ill. "We dedicate this concert to Mrs. Moring in the hope that she will get well," she said.

Then Katherine turned and, with great flair, began the performance. As the voices intoned the familiar Christmas hymns, her confidence rose. But one thought continued to nag her: *Can I keep them together for the finale?*

When the powerful opening to the "Hallelujah Chorus" burst from the organ, Katherine took a deep breath and raised her arms. There was an excruciating pause. Then she flung her arms wide—and heard the voices explode, every note in place, warm and confident. Mrs. Moring's students were summoning sounds so pure that Handel's long crescendo of "hallelujahs" seemed to soar to the rafters, touching ears and hearts with the sound of heaven itself.

When silence finally fell, the listeners rose and broke into applause, some weeping and others crowding forward to embrace the singers. Exhausted, Katherine felt a hug at her waist. It was the Morings' daughter, Elizabeth, embracing her as tightly as she could. Looking into the child's slate-blue eyes, Katherine was overcome with joy.

❉ ❉ ❉

That same night, less than a mile from the church, Danny Moring sat holding his wife's hand, the tape made by her students still playing. Allyson's condition remained hopeless. Danny didn't even know whether the news of the successful Christmas concert had penetrated her unconsciousness.

But slowly, remarkably, over the next few days, her systems began to stabilize. Lungs and kidneys started functioning. Allyson began to recover.

On Christmas morning, just 17 days after the concert, Allyson sat quietly in her own living room. Baby Robert squirmed in her lap as Danny and Elizabeth fetched presents from beneath the tree. Allyson was bone thin and exhausted, but her face wore a radiant smile.

Why she got well, or even when the precise turning point came, is not important to Allyson Moring. The key fact is that her long, tortured slumber was filled with music. "What I remember is music, music, music—the beautiful music and voices that I love."

Soon after Mrs. Moring got home, Katherine Allen and Jessica Boulware and several others from the choral group tapped gingerly on her door, bearing gifts and flowers. There was an explosion of emotion as the girls and Mrs. Moring hugged one another. She told the girls what she had told so many—that the entire experience has certified her faith in God's power through music and prayer and the wonderful capacity of young people.

Today Allyson Moring, completely recovered, is busy putting final touches on this year's Bishop England Christmas concert. "God wants me to be here," she says, "and that's a lot to live up to."

If the most precious of God's gifts is life, the Morings have realized a blessing every bit as special to them as

Allyson's recovery—a baby boy born to them in October, named Jonathon Tucker.

Merry Christmas, Mrs. Moring.

Henry Hurt

Henry Hurt writes about contemporary issues.

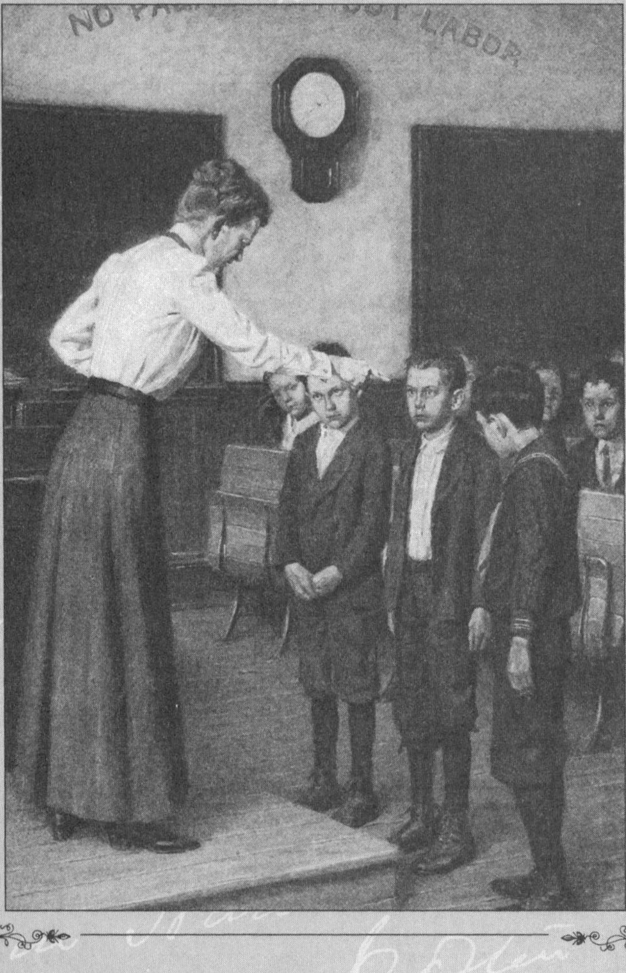

THE NIGHT THE
STARS SANG

---

*Parents are entrusted with one of the most
awesome responsibilities mankind can shoulder:
to shepherd awakening minds and hearts. This
development has no set timetable; it may occur
in childhood, youth, middle age, or the twilight
years, or it may never take place at all. One
never knows what the catalyst will be that sets
the stage for this miracle. Dorothy Canfield
Fisher, one of America's most beloved writers,
explores in this long-revered story just such an
awakening of what she poetically calls the "soul."*

*C*asually, not that she was especially interested, just to say something, she asked as she handed out the four o'clock pieces of bread and peanut butter, "Well, what Christmas songs are you learning in your room this year?"

There was a moment's pause. Then the three little boys, her own and the usual two of his playmates, told her somberly, first one speaking, then another, "We're not going to be let to sing." "Teacher don't want us in the Christmas entertainment." Their round, eight-year-old faces were grave.

"Well—!" said the mother. "For goodness' sake, why not?"

Looking down at his feet, her own small David answered sadly, "Teacher says we can't sing good enough."

"Well enough," corrected his mother mechanically.

"Well enough," he repeated as mechanically.

One of the others said in a low tone, "She says we can't carry a tune. She's only going to let kids sing in the entertainment that can carry a tune."

David, still hanging his head humbly, murmured, "She says we'd spoil the piece our class is going to sing."

Inwardly the mother broke into a mother's rage at the teacher. *So that's what she says, does she? What's she for, anyhow, if not to teach children what they don't know. The idea! As if she'd say she would teach arithmetic only to those who are good at it already.*

The downcast children stood silent. She yearned over their shame at failing to come up to the standards of their group. *Teachers are callous, that's what they are, insensitively callous. She is deliberately planting an inferiority feeling in them. It's a shame to keep them from going up on the plat-*

*form and standing in the footlights. Not to let them have their
share of being applauded! It's cruel.*

She drew in a deep breath, and put the loaf of bread
away. Then she said quietly, "Well, lots of kids your age
can't carry a tune. Not till they've learned. How'd you
like to practice your song with me? I could play the air
on the piano afternoons, after school. You'd get the
hang of it that way."

They brightened, they bit off great chunks of their
snacks, and said, thickly, that that would be swell. They
did not say they would be grateful to her, or regretted
being a bother to her, busy as she always was. She did
not expect them to. In fact it would have startled her if
they had. She was the mother of four.

So while the after-school bread-and-butter was being
eaten, washed down with gulps of milk, while the
November-muddy galoshes were taken off, the mother
pushed to the back of the stove the interrupted rice
pudding, washed her hands at the sink, looked into the
dining room where her youngest, Janey, was waking her
dolls up from naps taken in the dining-room chairs, and
took off her apron. Together the four went into the
living room to the piano.

"What song is your room to sing?"

"It came upon the midnight—" said the three little
boys, speaking at once.

"That's a nice one," she commented, reaching for the
battered songbook on top of the piano. "This is the way
it goes." She played the air, and sang the first two lines.
"That'll be enough to start on," she told them. *"Now—"*
she gave them the signal to start.

They started. She had given them food for body

and heart. Refreshed, heartened, with unquestioning confidence in a grown-up's ability to achieve whatever she planned, they opened their mouths happily and sang out.

> *It came upon the midnight clear*
> *That glorious song of old.*

They had evidently learned the words by heart from hearing them.

At the end of that phrase she stopped abruptly, and for an instant bowed her head over the keys. Her feeling about Teacher made a right-about turn. There was a pause.

But she was a mother, not a teacher. She lifted her head, turned a smiling face on the three bellowing children. "I tell you what," she said. "The way, really, to learn a tune, is just one note after another. The reason why a teacher can't get *everybody* in her room up to singing in tune is because she'd have to teach each person separately—unless they happen to be naturally good at singing. That would take too much time, you see. A teacher has such a lot of children to see to."

They did not listen closely to this. They were not particularly interested in having justice done to Teacher, since they had not shared the mother's brief excursion into indignation. But they tolerated her with silent courtesy. They were used to parents, teachers, and other adults, and had learned how to take with patience and self-control their constantly recurring prosy explanations of things that did not matter.

"Listen," said the mother, "I'll strike just the two first notes on the piano—'It came'—" She struck the notes, she sang them clearly. Full of good will the little boys sang with her. She stopped. Breathed hard.

"Not quite," she said, with a false smile, "pret-t-ty good. Close to it. But not quite, yet. I think we'd better take it *one* note at a time. Bill, *you* try it."

They had been in and out of her house all their lives, they were all used to her, none of them had reached the age of self-consciousness. Without hesitation, Bill sang, "I-i-it —" loudly.

After he had, the mother, as if fascinated, kept her eyes fixed on his still open mouth. Finally, "Try again," she said. "But first, *listen.*" Oracularly she told them, "Half of carrying a tune is listening first."

She played the note again. And again. And again. Then, rather faintly, she said, "Peter, you sing it now."

At the note emitted by Peter, she let out her breath, as if she had been under water and just come up. "Fine!" she said. "Now we're getting somewhere! David, your turn." David was her own. "Just that one note. No, not *quite*. A little higher. Not quite so high." She was in a panic. What could she do? "Wait," she told David. "Try just breathing it out, not loud at all. Maybe you can get it better."

❊ ❊ ❊

That evening when she told her husband about it, after the children had gone to bed, she ended her story with a vehement "You never heard anything like it in your life, Harry. Never. It was appalling! You can't *imagine* what it was!"

"Oh, yes I can too," he said over his temporarily

lowered newspaper. "I've heard plenty of tone-deaf kids hollering. I know what they sound like. There *are* people, you know, who really *can't* carry a tune. You probably never could teach them. Why don't you give it up?"

Seeing, perhaps, in her face the mulish mother-stubbornness, he said, with a little exasperation, "What's the use of trying to do what you *can't* do?"

That was reasonable, after all, thought the mother. *Yes, that was the sensible thing to do.* She would be sensible, for once, and give it up. With everything she had to do, she would just be reasonable and sensible about this.

So the next morning, when she was downtown doing her marketing, she turned in at the public library and asked for books about teaching music to children. Rather young children, about eight years old, she explained.

The librarian, enchanted with someone who did not ask for a light, easy-reading novel, brought her two books, which she took away with her.

At lunch she told her husband (there were just the two of them with little Janey; the older children had their lunch at school), "Musical experts say there really is no such thing as a tone-deaf person. If anybody seems so, it is only because he has not had a chance to be carefully enough trained."

Her husband looked at her quickly. "Oh, all right," he said, "all *right!* Have it your own way." But he leaned across to pat her hand. "You're swell," he told her. "I don't see how you ever keep it up as you do. My goodness, it's one o'clock already."

❄ ❄ ❄

During the weeks between then and the Christmas entertainment, she saw no more than he how she could ever
keep it up. The little boys had no difficulty in keeping it
up. They had nothing else to do at four o'clock. They
were in the indestructible age, between the frailness of
infancy and the taut nervous tensions of adolescence.
Wherever she led they followed her cheerfully. In that
period of incessant pushing against barriers which did not
give way, she was the one whose flag hung limp.

Assiduous reading of those two reference books on
teaching music taught her that there were other
approaches than a frontal attack on the tune they wanted
to sing. She tried out ear-experiments with them, of
which she would never have dreamed, without her
library books. She discovered to her dismay that sure
enough, just as the authors of the book said, the little
boys were musically so far below scratch that, without
seeing which piano keys she struck, they had no idea
whether a note was higher or lower than the one before
it. She adapted and invented musical "games" to train
their ear for this. The boys standing in a row, their backs
to the piano, listening to hear whether the second note
was "up hill or down hill" from the first note, thought it
as good a game as any other, rather funnier than most
because so new to them. They laughed raucously over
each other's mistakes, kidded and joshed each other, ran a
contest to see who came out best, while the mother,
aproned for cooking, her eye on the clock, got up and
down for hurried forays into the kitchen where she was
trying to get supper.

David's older brother and sister had naturally good ears for music. That was one reason why the mother had not dreamed that David had none. When the two older children came in from school, they listened incredulously, laughed scoffingly, and went off to skate, or to rehearse a play. Little Janey, absorbed in her family of dolls, paid no attention to these male creatures of an age so far from hers that they were as negligible as grown-ups. The mother toiled alone, in a vacuum, with nobody's sympathy to help her, her great stone rolling down hill as fast as she toilsomely pushed it up.

Not quite in a vacuum. Not even in a vacuum. Occasionally the others made a comment, "Gee, Mom, those kids are fierce. *You* can't do anything with them." "Say, Helen, an insurance man is coming to the house this afternoon. For heaven's sake keep those boys from screeching while he is here. A person can't hear himself think."

So, she thought, with silent resentment, her task was not only to give up her own work, to invent and adapt methods of instruction in an hour she could not spare, but also to avoid bothering the rest. After all, the home was for the whole family. They had the right to have it the background of what *they* wanted to do, needed to do. Only not she. Not the mother. Of course.

She faltered. Many times. She saw the ironing heaped high, or Janey was in bed with a cold, and as four o'clock drew near, she said to herself, *Now today I'll just tell the boys that I can not go on with this. We're not getting anywhere, anyhow.*

So when they came storming in, hungry and cheerful and full of unquestioning certainty that she would not

close that door she had half-opened for them, she laid
everything aside and went to the piano.

❄ ❄ ❄

As a matter of fact, they *were* getting somewhere. She had
been so beaten down that she was genuinely surprised at
the success of the exercises ingeniously devised by the
authors of those books. Even with their backs to the
piano, the boys could now tell, infallibly, whether a
second note was above or below the first one. Sure. They
even thought it distinctly queer that they had not been
able to, at first. "Never paid any attention to it, before,"
was their own accurate surmise as to the reason.

They paid attention now, their interest aroused by
their first success, by the incessant practicing of the
others in their classroom, by the Christmas-entertain-
ment thrill which filled the schoolhouse with suspense.
Although they were allowed no part in it, they also paid
close attention to the drill given the others, and sitting
in their seats, exiled from the happy throng of singers,
they watched how to march along the aisle of the
Assembly Hall, decorously, not too fast, not too slow,
and when the great moment came for climbing to the
platform how not to knock their toes against the steps.
They fully expected—wasn't a grown-up teaching
them?—to climb those steps to the platform with the
others, come the evening of the entertainment.

It was now not on the clock that the mother kept her
eye during those daily sessions at the piano, it was on
the calendar. She nervously intensified her drill, but she
remembered carefully not to yell at them when they

went wrong, not to screw her face into the grimace which she felt, not to clap her hands over her ears and scream, "Oh, horrible! *Why* can't you get it right!" She reminded herself that if they knew how to get it right, they would of course sing it that way. She knew (she had been a mother for sixteen years) that she must keep them cheerful and hopeful, or the tenuous thread of their interest and attention would snap. She smiled. She did not allow herself even once to assume the blighting look of impatience.

Just in time, along about the second week of December, they *did* begin to get somewhere. They could all sound—if they remembered to sing softly and to "listen to themselves"—a note, any note, within their range, she struck on the piano. Little Peter turned out, to his surprise and hers, to have a sweet clear soprano. The others were—well, all right, good enough.

They started again, very cautiously, to sing that tune, to begin with "It ca-ame—" having drawn a deep breath, and letting it out carefully. It was right. They were singing true.

She clapped her hands like a girl. They did not share her overjoyed surprise. That was where they had been going all the time. They had got there, that was all. What was there to be surprised about?

After that it went fast; the practicing of the air, their repeating it for the first skeptical, and then thoroughly astonished Teacher, their triumphant report at home, "She says we can sing it good enough. She says we can sing with the others. We practiced going up on the platform this afternoon."

Then the Christmas entertainment. The tramping of

class after class up the aisle to the moment of foot-lighted glory; the big eighth-graders' Christmas panto-mime, the first graders' wavering performance of a Christmas dance as fairies—or were they snowflakes? Or perhaps angels? It was not clear. They were tremen-dously applauded, whatever they were. The swelling hearts of their parents burst into wild hand-clapping as the first-graders began to file down the steps from the platform. Little Janey, sitting on her mother's lap, beat her hands together too, excited by the thought that next year she would be draped in white cheesecloth, would wear a tinsel crown and wave a star-tipped wand.

Then it was the turn of the third grade, the eight- and nine-year-olds, the boys clumping up the aisle, the girls swishing their short skirts proudly. The careful tiptoeing up the steps to the platform, remembering not to knock their toes on the stair treads, the two lines of round faces facing the audience, bland and blank in their ignorance of—*oh, of everything!* thought David's mother, her hand clutching her handbag tensely.

The crash from the piano giving them the tone, all the mouths open,

> *It came upo-on the midnight clear*
> *That glorious song of old.*

The thin pregnant woman sitting in front of the mother leaned to the shabbily dressed man next to her, with a long breath of relief. "They do real *good*, don't they?" she whispered proudly.

They did do real good. Teacher's long drill and hers had been successful. It was not howling, it was singing.

It had cost the heart's blood, thought the mother, of two women, but it was singing. It would never again be howling, not from those children.

It was even singing with expression—some. There were swelling crescendos, and at the lines

The world in solemn stillness lay
To hear the angels sing.

the child-voices were hushed in a diminuendo. Part of the mother's very life had been spent in securing her part of that diminuendo. She ached at the thought of the effort that had gone into teaching that hushed tone, of the patience and self-control and endlessly repeated persistence in molding into something shapely the boys' puppy-like inability to think of anything but aimless play. It had taken hours out of her life, crammed as it was far beyond what was possible with work that must be done. Done for other people. Not for her. Not for the mother.

This had been one of the things that must be done. And she had done it. There he stood, her little David, a fully accredited part of his corner of society, as good as anybody, the threat of the inferiority-feeling averted for this time, ready to face the future with enough self-confidence to cope with what would come next. The door had been slammed in his face. She had pushed it open, and he had gone through.

The hymn ended. The burst of parental applause began clamorously. Little Janey, carried away by the festival excitement, clapped with all her might—*learning the customs of her corner of society,* thought her mother, smiling tenderly at the petal-soft noiselessness of the tiny hands.

The third-graders filed down the steps from the platform and began to march back along the aisle. For a
moment, the mother forgot that she was no longer a
girl, who expected recognition when she had done
something creditable. David's class clumped down the
aisle. *Surely,* she thought, *David would turn his head to
where she sat and thank her with a look. Just this once.*

He did turn his head as he filed by. He looked full at
his family, at his father, his mother, his kid sister, his big
brother and sister from the high school. He gave them a
formal, small nod to show that he knew they were
there, to acknowledge publicly that they were his
family. He even smiled, a very little, stiffly, fleetingly.
But his look was not for her. It was just as much for
those of his family who had been bored and impatient
spectators of her struggle to help him, as for her who
had given part of her life to roll that stone up hill, a part
of her life she could never get back.

She shifted Janey's weight a little on her knee. Of
course. Did mothers ever expect to be thanked? They
were to accept what they received, without bitterness,
without resentment. After all, that was what mothers
worked for—not for thanks, but to do their job. The
sharp chisel of life, driven home by experience, flaked off
expertly another flint-hard chip from her blithe, selfish
girlhood. It fell away from the woman she was growing
to be, and dripped soundlessly into the abyss of time.

After all, she thought, hearing vaguely the seventh-
graders now on the platform (none of her four was in
the seventh grade), *David was only eight.* At that age they
were, in personality, completely cocoons, as in their
babyhood they had been physical cocoons. The time

had not come yet for the inner spirit to stir, to waken, to give a sign that it lived.

It certainly did not stir in young David that winter. There was no sign that it lived. The snowy weeks came and went. He rose, ravenously hungry, ate an enormous breakfast with the family, and clumped off to school with his own third-graders. The usual three stormed back after school, flinging around a cloud of overshoes, caps, mittens, windbreakers. For their own good, for the sake of their wives-to-be, for the sake of the homes which would be dependent on them, they must be called back with the hard-won, equable reasonableness of the mother, and reminded to pick up and put away. David's special two friends came to his house at four to eat her cookies, or went to each other's houses to eat other cookies. They giggled, laughed raucously, kidded and joshed each other, pushed each other around. They made snow-forts in their front yards, they skated with awkward energy on the place where the brook overflowed the meadow, took their sleds out to Hingham Hill for coasting, made plans for a shack in the woods next summer.

In the evening, if the homework had been finished in time, they were allowed to visit each other for an hour, to make things with Meccano, things which were a source of enormous pride to the eight-year-olds, things which the next morning fell over, at the lightest touch of the mother's broom. . . .

❄ ❄ ❄

David and Peter, living close to each other, shared the evening play-hour more often than the third boy who lived across the tracks. They were allowed to go by themselves, to each other's house, even though it was winter-black at seven o'clock. Peter lived on the street above theirs, up the hill. There was a short-cut down across a vacant lot, which was in sight of one or the other house, all the way. It was safe enough, even for youngsters, even at night. The little boys loved that downhill short-cut. Its steep slope invited their feet to fury. Never using the path, they raced down in a spray of snow kicked up by their flying overshoes, arriving at the house, their cheeks flaming, flinging themselves like cannon-balls against the kitchen door, tasting a little the heady physical fascination of speed, on which, later, as skiers, they would become wildly drunken.

"Sh! *David!* Not so *loud!*" his mother often said, springing up from her mending at the crash of the banged-open door. "Father's trying to do some accounts," or "Sister has company in the living room."

Incessant acrobatic feat—to keep five people of different ages and personalities, all living under the same roof, from stepping on each other's feet. Talk about keeping five balls in the air at the same time! That was nothing compared to keeping five people satisfied to live with each other, to provide each one with approximately what he needed and wanted without taking away something needed by one of the others. (Arithmetically considered, there were of course six people living under that roof. But she did not count. She was the mother. She took what she got, what was left. . . .)

That winter, as the orbits of the older children lay

more outside the house, she found herself acquiring a new psychological skill that was almost eerie. She could be in places where she was not, at all. She had an astral body which could go anywhere.* Anywhere, that is, where one of her five was. She was with her honey-sweet big daughter in the living room, playing games with high-school friends (was there butter enough, she suddenly asked herself, for the popcorn the young people would inevitably want, later?). She was upstairs where her husband sat, leaning over the desk, frowning in attentiveness at a page of figures—that desk-light was not strong enough. Better put the flood-light up there tomorrow. She was in the sun-porch of the neighbor's house, where her little son was bolting Meccano-strips together with his square, strong, not-very-clean hands. . . . She floated above the scrimmage in the high-school gym, where her first-born played basketball with ferocity, pouring out through that channel the rage of maleness constantly gathering in his big frame which grew that year with such fantastic rapidity that he seemed taller at breakfast than he had been when he went to bed. She sent her astral body upstairs to where her little daughter, her baby, her darling, slept with one doll in her arms, and three others on the pillow beside her. That blanket was not warm enough for Janey. When she went to bed, she would put on another one.

She was all of them. First one, then another. When was she herself? When did she have time to stretch *her* wings?

---

* Dorothy Canfield Fisher's use of the term "astral body" is not a New Age reference but an earlier era's symbolic way to describe a mother's intuition.

❄ ❄ ❄

One evening this question tried to push itself into her mind, but was swept aside by her suddenly knowing, as definitely as if she had heard a clock strike, or the door-bell ring, that the time had passed for David's return from his evening play-hour with Peter. She looked at her watch. But she did not need to. A sixth sense told her heart, as with a blow, that he should before this have come pelting home down the hill, plowing the deep snow aside in clouds, hurling himself against the kitchen door. He was late. Her astral self, annihilating time and space, fled out to look for him. He must have left the other house some time ago. Peter's mother always sent him home promptly.

She laid down the stocking she was darning, stepped into the dark kitchen, and put her face close to the window to look out. It was a cloudless cold night. Every detail of the back-yard world was visible, almost transparent, in the pale radiance that fell from the stars. Not a breath of wind. She could see everything: the garbage pail at the woodshed door, the trampled snow of the driveway, the clothes she had washed that morning and left on the line, the deep unbroken snow beyond the yard, the path leading up the hill.

Then she saw David. He was standing halfway down, as still as the frozen night around him.

But David *never* stood still.

Knee-deep in the snow he stood, looking all around him. She saw him slowly turn his head to one side, to the other. He lifted his face towards the sky. It was almost frightening to see *David* stand so still. What could he be looking at? What was there he could be seeing? Or hearing? For as she watched him, the notion crossed her mind that he seemed to be listening. But there was nothing to hear. Nothing.

She did not know what was happening to her little son. Nor what to do. So she did nothing. She stood as still as he, her face at the window, lost in wonder.

She saw him, finally, stir and start slowly, slowly down the path. But David *never* moved slowly. Had he perhaps had a quarrel with Peter? Had Peter's mother been unkind to him?

It could do no harm now to go to meet him, she thought, and by that time, she could not, anxious as she was, not go to meet him. She opened the kitchen door and stepped out into the dark, under the stars.

He saw her, he came quickly to her, he put his arms around her waist. With every fiber of her body which had borne his, she felt a difference in him.

She did not know what to say, so she said nothing.

It was her son who spoke. "It's so still," he said quietly in a hushed voice, a voice she had never heard before. "It's so still!"

He pressed his cheek against her breast as he tipped his head back to look up. "All those stars," he murmured dreamily, "they shine so. But they don't make a sound. They—they're *nice,* aren't they?"

He stood a little away from her to look up into her face. "Do you remember—in the song—'the world in solemn stillness lay'?" he asked her, but he knew she remembered.

The starlight showed him clearly, his honest, little-boy eyes wide, fixed trustingly on his mother's. He was deeply moved. But calm. This had come to him while he was still so young that he could be calmed by his mother's being with him. He had not known that he had an inner sanctuary. Now he stood in it, awe-struck at his first sight of beauty. And opened the door to his mother.

As naturally as he breathed, he put into his mother's hands the pure rounded pearl of a shared joy. "I thought I heard them singing—sort of," he told her.

Dorothy Canfield Fisher
(1879–1958)

Dorothy Canfield Fisher was born in Lawrence, Kansas, but wrote mainly from Arlington, Vermont. Fisher wrote more than forty books, including novels, short story collections, juvenile works, and nonfiction, and was considered one of the leading writers of her time. Among her books are *The Squirrel Cage* (1912), *The Bent Twig* (1915), *The Brimming Cup* (1921), and *The Home-Maker* (1924).

CHRISTMAS WITHOUT
GRANDMA KAY

---

*It was not going to be an easy Christmas, for
Grandma Kay had so recently left them. But the
family decided to make the most of it anyhow.*

Even to the three squeezes.

*O*K," I agreed with my husband, Ross. "We'll invite your family here for Christmas. But you know it's going to be hard for everyone since your mom passed away."

"I know," he said. "That's why we all need to be together."

I sort of agreed with him. But I knew I couldn't take Kay's place as hostess. I was still grieving myself and didn't feel I could be responsible for the emotional atmosphere on our first holiday without her.

I made all the preparations—cookies, decorations, presents—then welcomed Ross's family on Christmas Eve with open arms as I braced myself for a holiday punctuated by sorrow. That evening at church, our clan filled the entire back section. Afterwards, at home, the kids scampered upstairs and Ross shouted, "Five minutes!" The adults settled in the living room and Ross began to read from Luke 2.

At verse eight, our six-year-old, Rachel, appeared at the top of the stairs wearing her brother's bathrobe, a shawl over her head and carrying a stuffed lamb under her arm. She struck a pose and stared at the light fixture over the dining-room table, as if an angel had just appeared.

My father-in-law chuckled. "Look at her! You'd think she could really hear heavenly voices."

Next came Mary, one of my nieces, who'd donned the blue bridesmaid dress I wore in my sister's wedding. I knew then that the kids had gotten into my closet. The plastic baby Jesus fit nicely under the full skirt of the blue dress. My son, appearing as Joseph, discreetly turned his head as Mary "brought forth" her firstborn son on the living-room floor, wrapped him in a dish towel, and laid him in the laundry basket.

We heard a commotion as Ross turned to Matthew 2 and read the cue for the Magi. He repeated it, louder: "We saw His star in the east and have come to worship Him."

One of my junior high-age nephews whispered, "You go first!" and pushed his older brother out of the bedroom into full view. Slowly the ultimate wise man descended with Rachel's black tutu on his head and carrying a large bottle of canola oil.

The adults burst out laughing and I did, too, until I realized what he was wearing. It was a gold brocade dress with pearls and sequins that circled the neck and shimmered down the entire left side. Obviously the kids had gone through the bags I'd brought home after we'd cleaned out Kay's closet. Bags filled with shoes, hats, a few dresses, and some scarves that still smelled like her.

The laughter quickly diminished when my father-in-law said, "Hey! That's Kay's dress! What are you doing wearing her dress?"

Rachel looked at Grandpa from her perch at the top of the staircase. "Grandma doesn't mind if he uses it," she said. "I know she doesn't."

We all glanced silently at each other.

I didn't doubt that Rachel had an inside track into her grandma's heart. Kay had been there the day she was born, waiting all night in the hospital, holding a vase with two pink roses picked from her garden. She'd carried the roses through two airports and on the hour-long flight, telling everyone who she was going to see:

"My son, his wife, my grandson, and the granddaughter I've been waiting for."

I'd slept with the two pink roses on my nightstand and my baby girl next to me in her bassinet. When I awoke early in the morning to nurse my squirming, squalling infant, I noticed a red mark on her cheek. Was it blood? A birthmark I hadn't noticed before?

No, it was lipstick. Grandma Kay had visited her first granddaughter sometime during the night.

It was Grandma Kay who taught Rachel the three silent squeezes. A squeeze-squeeze-squeeze of the hand means, "I-love-you." My introduction to the squeezes was in the bride's dressing room on my wedding day. Kay slid past the wedding coordinator and photographer. In all the flurry, she quietly slipped her soft hand into mine and squeezed it three times. After that, I felt the silent squeezes many times. We all did.

When we got the call last year that Kay had gone into a diabetic coma, Ross caught the next plane home. Our children and I prayed this would only be a close call, like so many others the past two years. But Kay didn't come out of it this time. A week later, we tried to accept the doctor's diagnosis that it was only a matter of days. The children seemed to understand that all we could do was wait.

One night that week, Rachel couldn't sleep. I brought her to bed with me but she wouldn't settle down. Crying, she said she wanted to talk to her grandma.

"Just have Daddy put the phone up to her ear," she pleaded. "I know she'll hear me."

It was 10:30 P.M. I called the hospital and asked for Kay's room. My husband answered at her bedside. I watched my daughter sit up straight and take a deep breath.

"OK, Rachel," my husband said. "You'll have to talk loud because there are noisy machines helping Grandma breathe."

"Grandma, it's me, Rachel," she shouted. "I wanted to tell you good night. I'll see you in heaven."

Rachel handed me the phone and nestled down under the covers. "Oh," she said, springing up. "Tell Daddy to give Grandma three squeezes for me."

Two days later, Grandma Kay died. She had left clear instructions to the family: she wanted to be cremated and her ashes scattered over the Pacific Ocean, whose waves she had gazed at every day from her kitchen window.

Rachel sat with her cousins during the memorial service and I couldn't help but notice her unusual calm and poise. She told everyone, "Grandma is going to see Noah and the real Rachel and David, but not Goliath, I don't think."

When we boarded the chartered yacht in Newport Beach to carry out Kay's wishes, the cousins all sported pudgy, orange life jackets and nibbled chips and M&M's. It was a painfully gorgeous summer evening and I missed Kay so much. But saying good-bye to her as the sun set and the brisk ocean wind flew against our faces was much sweeter than huddling around a sealed box. In her death, as in life, she thought first of what others would enjoy.

Earlier that afternoon, with a dozen flower baskets encircling her, Rachel had secretly instructed her cousins to "pick a bouquet for Grandma to take on the boat." As the yacht sped out to sea, the cousins retrieved their flowers and tossed them into the water in turn, saying good-bye to Grandma Kay that sun-kissed Southern California evening.

I bit my lower lip when I saw Rachel's bouquet. It was centered with two pink roses. She tossed it overboard, the last one to say good-bye.

Now, Christmas Eve, in our snow-covered house, Rachel was the first to welcome Grandma's memory into our celebration.

"Really, Grandpa," she continued to plead, "Grandma wouldn't mind."

We all knew Rachel was right. Grandma Kay wouldn't have cared if her grandchildren found delight in anything that belonged to her. If the dress had been embroidered with pure 14-karat gold, Grandma Kay wouldn't have minded a bit.

Grandpa nodded. The pageant continued. The next wise man paraded down the stairs, stumbling on his too-big bathrobe, a towel wrapped around his head and bearing a jumbo-sized Lawry's Seasoned Salt. He laid it at the laundry basket.

My husband read about the shepherds returning, "glorifying and praising God for all the things they had heard and seen, just as they had been told."

Then the cast took a bow and scrambled for the kitchen where they fought over lighting the candle on Jesus' birthday cake.

When we started singing "Happy Birthday" to Jesus, I looked down at the little shepherdess standing next to me. *Maybe Grandpa was right. Maybe she really did hear heavenly voices.*

Then Rachel's small, warm hand nuzzled its way into

mine. I knew Grandma Kay was there, too, when I felt three silent squeezes.

Robin Jones Gunn

Robin Jones Gunn grew up in Southern California but now lives and writes near Portland, Oregon. She is the author of forty-six books, and over 3,000,000 copies of her books have sold world-wide. She has a wide teen audience for her various book series.

Louis Arthur Cunningham

AND YOU SHALL
RECEIVE

*Each had—before the terrible war—acknowledged love
for the other. And then each had rejected the other.*

*So why, when it was all over, did their hearts
continue to yearn for the impossible?*

❄ ❄ ❄

*This is one of the greatest Canadian love stories to
come out of World War II.*

*H*e had vowed long ago that he was done with all sentiment, all that the cynic in him called "sweetness and light," all faith in woman, all belief in the ultimate justice of God—for a woman had let him down badly and God had let so many good men die. For what?

For this, perhaps, thought Kilmer now, on Christmas Eve, as he walked the streets, gay and crowded, of his own city, with war behind him, all its ugliness and its pain.

For this, perhaps, that children's eyes might shine with that heavenly light as they gazed on the color and beauty of the Christmas trees in the shop windows; for this, that men and women might meet and shake hands and kiss and be glad and say, "Merry Christmas—many of them," and go smiling on their way; for this, that from the cathedral as he passed the glory of the "Adeste" might stream out as the choir practiced for the Midnight Mass—

No more faith in woman—yet he had in his wanderings, by some remaining tenderness, passed the house where she lived. He knew the place, the old Courtney house on Peel Street, where Jeff Courtney had taken her as a bride, where now she lived as his widow with his son, a child of four.

"Don't be a fool, Kilmer," he had told himself, passing the house on Peel Street, seeing the holly-wreaths with their red ribbons on door and window. "Don't go back for more punishment. All that was between Alison Chanter and you ended five years ago in a garden by the Thames. You said goodbye; there wasn't any more, there never can be any more. Get out of this town now—go west, go anywhere, but never back to her. She left you in that garden; we had quarreled, yes, but still she left you thinking, *She'll come back. We love each other. We'll always love.* But she never did come back. She went home, back to Canada, and in less than a month was married to Jeff Courtney—Jeff who died a year afterwards in Iceland waters. There's nothing there for you, fool—nothing of the Alison who walked in these places with you long ago—"

❄ ❄ ❄

Still he passed her house, slowly, and then trudged by the church and the convent-school at whose gates he had waited for her so many afternoons—Alison of the red curls and deep blue eyes and small fair form. "That was long ago," he muttered. "That was long ago, and in another land, and that girl—there's nothing of her now—"

Still he kept walking along the familiar streets, past the old familiar places—the common with its snow-piled walks, its frozen fountain, its huge Christmas tree around which, these nights, the carol-singers gathered. He stood among the crowd by the tree now in the winter dusk and the lights were popping out all around the common—blue, red, yellow, shimmering and shifting and turning the smoke-smeared snow into a white and sequined beauty. Then the lights on the great spruce bloomed out suddenly and the big star on its tip seemed to blaze up to the silent ones that watched above, and some of the harshness, some of the war-graven lines, seemed to melt from Ives Kilmer's face, and he smiled when the voices, as of angels, filled the night and the heavens with the sweeping beauty of the Westminster Carol—

Voices we have heard on high
Lightly singing o'er the plain,
And the mountains in reply
Echo back their joyous strain—
Gloria in excelsis Deo!

Kilmer's look was good then and his tall, spare figure, in the unaccustomed gray suit and Burberry and soft grey hat, stood straight and shoulder-square amongst the crowd—and Alison Courtney, who had been Alison Chanter, seeing him then, clutched young Jeff's hand till he tried to withdraw it and in her heart a song awoke that had been dead a long, long time.

"It's Ives," she said softly, but it was as if she was telling it to the world and the heavens. "It's Ives Kilmer, young Jeff. He's home again. He's here—" And then her mouth quivered and shook and all the lights and the tree and the snow made only a blur and she seemed to stand afar off and see a girl who was Alison Chanter praying for a crumb of forgiveness, a crust of kindness, found herself absurdly saying Masefield's words— "The beggar with the saucer in his hand asks only a penny of the passing crowd—"

"He refused me the crumb, the crust, the penny," she found herself saying then. "I'm too proud to ask again. I humbled myself once before him, I practically begged him to marry me and I'd stay in England or go home, whatever he wished. It was the unconditional surrender of Alison—and he sat like a stone and never said a word—not one word of forgiveness for the quarrel we'd had a week before—nothing whatever of the thing I'd asked of him—a thing so against my pride that I could not even face him but stood behind his shoulder, there in the dusk of the garden. I hated him then, when after I'd told him I'd go home and marry Jeff, he still didn't try to keep me. But I can't hate him now—maybe I never really did. But I'm proud now; I'll never crawl to him again."

✳ ✳ ✳

But her eyes were a glory when they met Kilmer's, and she was glad that when they moved together and met and gave hand to hand, it was in the shadows on the edge of the crowd.

"Welcome home, Ives," she said. "I could scarcely believe it was you. But then, nice things come with Christmas trees."

He didn't speak for a moment or so; just stood with her gray gloved hand in his big fingers, still brown and hard from the sun and mud of the Flemish fields. Then he said, "You're lovelier than you ever were, Alison— so lovely—" Then he fetched himself up, remembering old things, harsh things, and said, "This is your boy."

"Yes." Alison's voice had lost some of its warmth too. "This is young Jeff. Say hello to Captain Kilmer, Jeff. He's an old friend."

Big eyes looked earnestly up at Ives and a small voice piped hello, the eyes never wavering from Kilmer's face. Kilmer thought, *Darn it, why does he have to have eyes like that, soft and wistful as a young collie's—lost eyes. He has no father, no man in his life. And he might have been mine; we might have done together all the things I planned to do—fish-ing, hunting in the autumn woods, ice-boating, learning to live, both of us. . . . But he's not mine. She walked out on me without giving me another chance, and made a life of her own. Well, she has something left of hers, but there's nothing at all left of mine.*

"Eh?" He started. He had been hearing Alison's low, husky voice, but not the words it was saying.

She laughed and there was a sudden pain in his heart: no other woman ever laughed like that—a rare, sweet sound. "You were dreaming, Ives. You didn't hear a word I said. I asked you if you were home for good."

"Home? Here—oh, no. I had a few things to attend to. I'm selling the house and then—"

"Where then, Ives?"

He shook his head. "I don't really know yet. I have no one of my own, you know—no one who cares what I do or where I go."

She winced a little. He knew it, but he didn't care. Once there had been so much, so very much between them. Through this same common they had walked, under the great maples and balm o' Gilead in summer, between the high-piled snow in winter. He had carried her books from school, so many days, and here one September night—the night before he left for college—in the moon-dappled shadow, he had kissed her and said, "You're mine, Alison—always mine," and she had answered, unhesitant, "Always yours, Ives." Then the years took them in turn to London, Alison to study, Ives soon afterwards to fight in a war—and in England the dream had ended. And you can't relive a dream.

The choristers were singing an old Welsh carol now:

Deck the halls with boughs of holly,
Fa-la-la-la-la-la-la-la-la.
Now's the season to be jolly,
Fa-la-la-la-la-la-la-la-la.

They stood silent, not knowing what to say, feeling the uselessness of small talk, the hopelessness of anything more grave.

"It's time for us to go." There was no life in her voice. "I promised Jeff I'd bring him to hear the Christmas carols. We didn't have them through the war. There was no tree, no lights, on account of the blackout. He never heard them before. He thinks the choir boys are angels." She smiled at Ives and he smiled back boyishly: once he'd stood there with Alison and "trolled out the ancient carol."

"You're remembering, Ives."

"No—no, Alison—trying to forget. Those times don't seem real to me any more. Here for a little while tonight, maybe—but—"

"I know."

They walked through the common, along the gaily lighted streets, then into the darker, quieter ones. Young Jeff's steps lagged. He'd had quite a day—an interview with Santa Claus, visits to many Christmas trees, then hearing the angels sing. He was glad when the big man picked him up and perched him on a shoulder that was like a rock. He put his small arms around Ives Kilmer's neck. "I like you," he said sleepily. "My own father is dead."

Ives did not look at Alison; he saw the white of her teeth as they caught her lip. His own eyes felt funny and a lot of things stirred in him that he had sworn never again to let awaken—emotions that could do things to a man. He was glad when they turned into Peel Street and he saw the lights in the windows glowing soft and red out on the snow.

He set Jeff down firmly and took off his hat, holding out his hand to Alison. She looked at him piteously for a moment, then her mouth stiffened and her small shoulders squared under the silver raccoon stole.

"Thank you, Ives. You'll—I'll be seeing you again. You won't come in—"

"Thank you, Alison. I'd better be on my way. It's been good seeing you, too, and your son. We'll meet again some day, I hope—"

She didn't answer. She took the little boy in her arms and carried him up the steps. Ives saw the door open and caught a glimpse of shiny wood and soft warm lights; then the door closed behind her, behind all he had ever loved or ever would love.

The street seemed bleak and the wind was sharp and searching. He had a wild impulse to dash up the steps and go in after her and take her in his arms and put his mouth against hers and stay that way forever. . . .

The impulse died. There was nothing in it. He was just kidding himself. Their roads had parted long ago; they hadn't really converged or, if so, only briefly.

He turned away. Under the street lamp his feet slowed to a stop. He looked back once more at the holly-wreathed windows and fell deeper into loneliness. He thought he saw the shadow of Alison there in the lighted pane. *Five years is too long,* he thought—*far too long. We can't pick up those lovely threads again—not with any hope of completing the pattern. It's been lost. Better not try at all.*

He went back to the hotel and ate a tasteless dinner and sat for a while dreaming, thinking that a hotel lobby on Christmas Eve was the loneliest place a lonely man could select. The emptiness of his life impressed itself deeper upon him; there was no warmth, no loving-kindness in it. He thought of friends who had joined the silent orders of monks, thought of how he'd pitied them; now he began to understand them.

Alison—Alison, he thought; *if I go back to her, if she'd have me again, there'd always be Jeff Courtney's ghost there with us and I'd never know that it was really love she gave me. No, she must have given her only real love to him. I'd be just another man to her—and once I loved her. Once? I love her now more than I ever did.*

❈ ❈ ❈

Midnight found him again walking the streets of the town, mingling with the current of people bound for church, thinking of the many Christmas Eves he had known, of Midnight Mass in the catacombs of Rome, in the little town of Bethlehem. The air was still, frosty; the stars never so bright in the deep blue sky, the aurora played its spotlights on the world.

At the Cathedral door he hesitated, listening to the prelude to "Messa Angelorum," the "Mass of the Angels."

"Ah, well!" he muttered. "Once more—I'll go once more. After all, it's Christmas."

He went up the side aisle to the pew Kilmers had sat

in for generations. He entered it and knelt and, as of old, turned his head to the transept, to the pew directly across the aisle—and saw her kneeling there, a blue halo hat crowning her dark red hair, framing a face that was to him always a madonna's face.

Her eyes strayed from the altar and met his briefly and her full lips curved a very little, then moved again in prayer. "Dear God!" she prayed. "Send Ives back to me. Don't let him go away. I need him. I always needed him. I'm so alone now, and my pride is gone. Bring him back to me. Bring him back to me."

Through the glory of the mass she prayed, thinking of the words, "Ask, and you shall receive." She had never asked much for herself. Pride and pique had driven her into a marriage which was not what she would have had with Kilmer. "I love him"—and it was a prayer. "God, I love him. Send him back to me."

The crowds streamed out of the church. Ives was at her shoulder, his hand upon her arm. In the shadow of the great buttress, he took her in his arms and kissed her and said, "Merry Christmas, Alison. Merry Christmas, my own, my own."

Her mouth trembled under his kiss and her arms were tight about his neck. Then he released her and they walked home through the silent streets, saying nothing, happy in each other, in their hearts a wondrous peace.

"You'll let me come in with you?" he said when they reached her house.

She only smiled at him and clung to his hand. They went in and stood before the fire in the living-room, looking down at the embers. Outside the wind made a weird keening and the town clock chimed out the half hour after one.

He drew her close to him, looking down at the shadowed planes of her face. "So you *do* love me, Alison—you *do* want me back," he said softly.

"How can you be so sure, Ives?"

"I heard you asking God to send me back to you."

She drew slowly away from him. "You—you *heard* me."

"There in the church tonight."

"You heard me when I was praying—you *couldn't* have. You—why, you couldn't hear me the night in the garden in England when I asked you aloud, almost begged you, to marry me."

"You asked me . . . *what?*"

"To marry me. I came close, stood behind you . . . but you were deaf to me that night."

"Right," he said. "I *was* deaf. Concussion. I'd been knocked over in the blitz, the day after we quarreled. Not hurt, but I was deaf for months. I didn't know you came back to the garden! No wonder you hated me—even enough to marry Jeff. But the same thing that took you away from me gave you back. I could read your lips tonight. I learned that trick in my deafness. I heard you say, 'Send him back to me.' I heard you say you loved me. And I was so happy—so glad. I believed again in the goodness of women and in the great kindness of God."

She came again, slowly, close into his arms and rested her head on his shoulder. His hand stroked the thick braids of her hair. The fire flickered low, the wind's keening had a softer tone, and now they could hear the music the stars make on this night.

Louis Arthur Cunningham
(1900–1954)

Louis Arthur Cunningham of Saint John, New Brunswick, was one of the most popular and prolific Canadian authors of his time, writing more than thirty novels and five hundred short stories. Fascinated by the geography and history of the Maritime provinces, he set much of his fiction in the Maritimes, as well as writing a great deal of regional nonfiction.

COLIN'S
CHRISTMAS CANDLE

Colin's father had been due home a week ago, but still no ship's sails appeared on the gray horizon.

It was on Christmas Eve that an idea suddenly came to the boy.

*C*olin walked slowly home from school, scuffing his feet as he crossed the hills of the little Irish fishing village. It did not seem like Christmas Eve. Perhaps this was because it had not yet snowed.

But Colin knew there was another reason why it did not seem like Christmas—a reason he did not dare even whisper in his heart.

He looked across the valley toward the lead-colored sea. There was not a speck of a ship on the horizon. There had been none for seven days now. And seven days ago his father's fishing schooner had been due home.

"I'll bring you a sheepdog pup from the Shetland Isles," Colin's father had called the morning he left. "You'll have it a week before Christmas, I am certain."

But it was already Christmas Eve. Colin looked toward the lighthouse, high on the hill. Seven days ago a north gale had short-circuited the lighthouse wires and had snuffed out the great light. For seven days there had been no light to guide a schooner home.

Colin pushed open the door of his mother's cottage. He heard her moving in the kitchen. "We'll need more peat for the fire, Colin," she said as she came into the front room. "It's nearly burned itself out, and it's nearly time to light the candle for the Christ Child."

"I'm not caring much about lighting a candle, Mother," he said.

"I know, for I'm not caring much either," replied his mother. "But everybody in Ireland lights a candle on Christmas Eve. Even when there's sadness in the house, you must light the candle. It is a symbol that your house and heart are open to poor strangers. Come now, I've two candles, one for each of us. If you gather some peat, we'll be ready for supper soon."

Colin went outside and hitched a basket to the donkey's back. He led the animal up the hill a way, so that he could gather the peat. "I'm not caring much about lighting a candle," he said as he glanced toward the lighthouse, "when there's not so much as a beam of light to guide a schooner home." The donkey shook his head and brayed sadly, almost as if he understood.

But while he was staring at the lighthouse, Colin had an idea. It hit him like a gust of wind, touching the top of his head and spreading down until his whole spine tingled.

He turned on his heels and started running up the long hill. When he came to the lighthouse he pounded on the door. Mr. Duffy, the keeper, padded across the room inside and opened the door a crack.

"What's got into you, young fellow, startling an old man like me—and on Christmas Eve, too?"

"Mr. Duffy," gasped Colin, "how did you light the lighthouse before electricity was put in? Could you do it again?"

"Why, by the oil lamp that's buried in the cellar. Now what wild thing have ye in mind? There's no oil kept here now." Mr. Duffy stared at Colin and then lowered his voice. "Sure, 'tis your father you're thinking of, if he's one of those on the lost schooner . . ."

"Would kerosene light the lamp?"

"Well, I suppose," Mr. Duffy mused, "although I've

never heard of its being used. But don't go getting any ideas in your head, lad. I'd like to see anyone find a quart of oil in this village, much less enough to . . ."

Colin was gone before Mr. Duffy could finish his sentence.

Down, down the hill he ran, back to the cottage. Quickly he gathered four pails from the kitchen and darted for the door. His mother ran after him to the steps. "Colin, 'tis time to light . . . Colin!" But he was gone.

Colin knew that a candle in an Irish home on Christmas Eve meant that any stranger coming to the door would be welcomed and given whatever he asked. It was five o'clock now and he could see candles beginning to glow in every cottage in the valley below him. He didn't stop running until he came to the first house.

"Could you spare me but half a cup of kerosene from your lamp?" he asked. "Have you any kerosene in your cellar?" Colin went to every house where a candle shone in the window.

In one hour he had filled two pails. Slowly and painfully he carted them, one by one, up to the lighthouse door.

He knocked. Mr. Duffy appeared, and stared.

"What manner of miracle is this?" he asked. "This is enough to keep the lamp burning for the night."

"I'll get more yet," Colin shouted, as he started down the hill. "It's still early."

After two more long hours, Colin had gathered two more pails of oil. When he was halfway up the hill for the second time, he saw the tower suddenly flicker with light. A great beam spread out over the valley and stretched toward the dark heart of the sea. Mr. Duffy had lighted the lamp!

When Colin reached home it was very late. His mother jumped from her seat near the fire.

"Colin, where have you been? You've had no supper, nor lighted your candle!"

"I've lighted a candle, Mother, and a big one! It's a secret, and I can't tell you yet. But it was a huge candle indeed!"

After that, Colin ate his supper and went quietly to bed.

He dreamed all night of candles, and fishing schooners, and kegs and kegs of oil. Then a great shouting aroused him from his sleep.

"The ship has come in! The ship has come in!" It seemed as if a hundred voices were spinning in his head. "'Twas the light, it was, they say—the light that Mr. Duffy lighted. They were but ten miles out all week after the storm, just drifting in the fog."

Colin opened his eyes. He saw that dawn was breaking and that his mother was standing at the door. People were milling outside the cottage. He bounded from bed and pulled on his clothes. He ran to the door and looked toward the harbor. It was true! There was the schooner with its rigging standing out black as coal against the gray of the sea.

Colin darted across the yard and raced for the harbor. He felt a moist wind on his face. It was beginning to snow. Oh, it was Christmas all right, falling from heaven and right into his heart!

Barbara Raftery

Barbara Raftery wrote for children's and popular magazines during the mid-twentieth century.

Esther Chapman Robb

THE WHITE SHAWL

---

*Their marriage on the rocks because of conflicting
career tracks, this was to be their last Christmas
together. Somehow, some way, at some time,
they'd have to tell the entire family. The big question
was—how?*

*Although this story goes back a number of years,
the dilemma is one almost every husband and wife
have to face sooner or later. Without a compromise,
another marriage will be history.*

*O*ut of the long silence, cold and smothering as the snowstorm itself, Laurel asked, "Are we here?" and rubbed impatiently with her small gloved hand at the misted car window.

"Right," said Stephen, relieved that she had spoken, but uncertain as to how to reach her remoteness with words. Words—always the wrong ones—there had been far too many of them already. Through the arc which the windshield wiper had labored to keep clear for him all the long drive from the city, he watched the white road slanting steeply down to the long-pointed stars in the snow which were the lights of Glen Mills.

"Four hours of it," he said unhappily. "I wish we— I wish I hadn't come. I ought to have taken the train from St. Paul as I planned in the first place."

"And leave me to break it all alone?" Laurel demanded.

"You'll know how to put it; I won't. What a sour note for Christmas Eve! Well—guess I'll stop by Lindstrom's and tell Pete to come for me by ten of eleven—"

"But of course I'll drive you down," she said quickly.

"No, thanks. I'll say good-bye to you at the house."

"As you like," she returned, lifting her chin slightly. "Have you any objection to taking the car yourself, and leaving it at the station?"

"I have. It's *your* car, and you'll need it tomorrow."

"It's your car just as much as it is mine!"

Because there was a break in her voice, Stephen said brusquely, "Let's not go over that again. Well . . . shall we stop downtown and get a bite? It's late, and your father likes his dinner early."

"That would hurt Grace's feelings; she'll have kept something hot for us."

"Just as you say." The next words came out before he could call them back: "It won't be the same without your mother."

"No," said Laurel in a low, tense voice, "Christmas will never be the same again."

Christmas was the one thing Laurel allowed herself to be sentimental about, Stephen reminded himself. When her sister's letter had come proposing Christmas as usual, she had agreed that Mother would wish it so, that Father would be looking for them all. Resisting the well-meant efforts of his children to dislodge him, Mr. Dean insisted upon fending for himself in the old house, with the occasional heavy-handed ministrations of Grace Bloomberg. Grace would do her devoted best, but Stephen was convinced that this attempt at a family Christmas would be a painful experience for them all.

He had deeply loved Laurel's gentle and gracious mother. She had treated him like one of her own sons, so that the ache of homelessness in his heart had some-how eased. It seemed to him that his own family, lost to him so early by death, would have been like the Deans; that this home was actually one he had known and loved long since. This little town, half-asleep by the river since the passing of the sawmills, reminded him that his people, too, had been builders of the West. To such a frontier as this had trekked his pioneering great-grandfather to keep store. . . .

At the state university, where his guardian-cousin in the East had sent him because Stephen's father had grad-uated there, he had met and loved Laurel Dean. She was the vivid, lively type to whom "quiet" lads like him were inevitably attracted, tireless in activity and insatiable in ambition.

It hadn't been fair of him to expect that Laurel would be like her mother. She was a modern girl with a modern profession—photography. Becoming something of a vogue with her character portraits, she couldn't consider giving up her work for marriage. Stephen, trying to be modern and realistic, had given in, not anticipating how he would come to feel about it. Laurel Dean Donaldson was a personage, but Mrs. Stephen Brooks Donaldson was a young woman nobody knew.

Since boyhood his real interest had been hardware. Laurel had thought his bringing home gadgets—beet slicers, door-stops, lemon squeezers—very funny, and passed them around among their friends, saying lightly, "If I could only keep Steve out of hardware stores—" Then had come the chance to be manager of the new store the Hartwell Hardware was about to open in Willetts, North Dakota. In great excitement he tried to explain to Laurel how he felt about it. "You see, Lollie, I'll never be anything but a washout selling bonds. I never feel sure of them. I need to sell something solid over a counter. I need to live in a little place where I can chew the fat with my neighbors and look at the sky and wonder whether we'll have it clear for threshing."

Laurel had flamed, "But my work, Steve! All I've built up. . . ."

"Lots of pictures to be taken in Dakota, Lollie. Wheat fields waving to the sky, home-places, Scandinavian farmers, wives, youngsters—"

For a moment Laurel looked as though she might be

seeing all those pictures waiting to be taken. Then she brushed them away with a weary little gesture across her eyes. "But I couldn't afford to close my studio; I make . . ."

"Don't say, 'more than you'! It's like poison to me. I see you getting the everlasting jitters working too hard, and I'm getting them, too, watching you drive yourself, and kicking myself because I don't take better care of you. This way, with expenses down and work I know I could do, because I'd like it, I could pay all our bills myself. It would mean a lot to me."

"Don't be mid-Victorian, Steve," Laurel had said in that brittle way that was growing on her. "Of all places, North Dakota!"

"What do you really *know* about North Dakota? It's coming back fast from the dust storms. The farmers haven't bought a tool or a machine for so long that everything is broken or lost or worn out. They'll need wire and nails and paint. The wives will be asking for radios and vacuum cleaners and washing machines."

He hadn't been able to make her see that opportunity was knocking at his door. Very well, he'd go to Willetts by himself! Thinking back, he wondered how it had been possible for two who loved each other to say such two-edged and bitter things. All their bridges were burned—except one. There remained only the task of telling the family.

When the Hartwell Company had asked him how soon he could go out to Willetts, he had told them, "Immediately." No, he didn't care about waiting until after Christmas. Then Laurel had asked him, as a favor, to go to Glen Mills with her for Christmas Eve, pleading that the explanations she would have to make for his absence would add too heavy a burden to a holiday that would be difficult enough. If Steve were present, even for four hours, the break wouldn't seem so final.

From Lindstrom's little shack by the river, they climbed the bluff again to the older residence section. At the corner of Maple and St. Croix, a rambling white house with a narrow, slender-columned porch cast rectangles of yellow light upon the snow. The bridal-wreath bushes were bending low with a heavier bloom than they had borne in May. The walk to the front door had been recently shoveled clean, but it was filling in again rapidly.

"The boys used to groan because we lived on the corner, and they had to shovel both walks," Laurel remembered audibly. As they scraped their snow-packed feet on the wire mat, the door popped open, and Stephen and Laurel were suddenly in the warm, bright hall under the prismed chandelier. There was the fragrance of coffee, and a confusion of welcoming voices, subdued from the hilarious shouts of other years.

Mr. Dean, his white hair a little long over the velvet collar of his dressing-jacket, his eyes bright brown under brushy white brows, came forward with quiet satisfaction. "Lollie! Steve! I told them you'd make it! Radio says the driving's bad, but I knew a little old-fashioned Minnesota weather couldn't keep you from coming home for Christmas."

Laurel kissed the cheek he stooped to give her, then turned abruptly to the far end of the hall. Laying her modish little hat on the marble shelf of the walnut hat rack, she stood there for a moment before the mirror, pushing up the russet waves of her hair. Eyes, lashes, brows were all of the same vibrant shade, very lovely against the creamy pallor of her skin. *Too pale tonight,* thought Stephen, and followed her quick, seeking glance into the sitting room. It traveled over the homely clutter of Victorian and Mission pieces until it found a brown wicker rocker. Over the high back of this chair lay a folded square of white wool. Laurel caught her lower lip briefly, then turned to join the family.

Suddenly, with creaking jerks, the double doors of the dining room were pulled apart, and there stood Grace Bloomberg, a durable-looking woman of more than middle age. Beaming and nodding, she wiped her red hands on her white apron, and held out first the left and then the right in awkward welcome.

"I wouldn't dish up till you come, Lollie," she said with her high-pitched, apologetic giggle. "Ain't it the limit how I can't never remember to say, 'Dinner's served,' like you learned me? Anyway, 'sall on!'"

With all its extra leaves inserted, the table stretched the length of the wood-paneled dining room. Mr. Dean, at the head, lifted dish covers and pronounced, "Good: baked potatoes and dried beef gravy. You can't beat that combination. You were all raised on it." Then, with a glance at the closed door into the kitchen, he added, "Well, Grace does her best, but no one can make dried beef gravy as your mother could."

"She always frizzled it in plenty of butter first," sister Helen said from mother's place. Then, flushing because she had spoken so matter-of-factly, she bowed her head quickly, pressing a hand on the child seated on either side of her to ensure quiet while grandfather asked the blessing.

"Still the priest in his own household," thought Stephen, only half-hearing the familiar, sonorous words of the grace: "Bless this food to our use and us to Thy service."

There were six children at table. Helen and Albert Tupper had four: Jessie, a solemn-eyed little girl with long brown braids; Edward, a snub-nosed lad with a gap in his front teeth; David and Jonathan, the four-year-old twins who could not be trusted to sit together. Norman Dean and his shy Swedish wife, Inga, had beaten the snowstorm down from Duluth. Their eldest, Carl, blue-eyed and flaxen-haired, sat high on the old *Webster's Dictionary,* while the fourteen-month-old baby girl occupied the highchair and busily plastered her fat pink cheeks with cereal.

After dinner Helen offered to help Inga get her babies to bed, remaining upstairs to make up the cots mother had bought for Laurel's house parties and kept to be ready for the visits of the grandchildren. In the sheer black dress into which she had changed for the evening, Laurel gathered the other children around her and read to them *The Birds' Christmas Carol.* The turbulent twins ceased their puppyish wrestling on the worn carpet, and edged closer until they were leaning against her knees. Edward lay on his stomach at her feet, chin cupped in his stubby hands. Stephen, watching them from across the sitting room, saw Laurel's arm in its long, graceful sleeve reach out to draw in self-conscious little Jessie. It was a pity, he felt sharply, that there was no place in

Laurel's crowded life for children of her own. She would have loved them. . . .

Closing the book now, Laurel cried gaily enough, "To bed with you, darlings! Just think, Jessie, next Christmas, when you're twelve, you will be allowed to join the trimmers of the tree."

With the children safely out of the way, there was feverish activity in the sitting room. The tree had to be dragged in from the back porch and shaken free of snow; the tree-stand had to be brought up from the basement; the attic ransacked for the boxes of trimmings; the linen closet turned out for a sufficiently worn sheet. Of all such details sister Helen was in command. Tirelessly she ran upstairs and down, protesting that it would help her "reduce," and holding up a warning finger to remind loud talkers that there were sleeping babies.

At the quieter end of the room, Stephen talked with Albert Tupper, a plain, thick-set man with sandy hair and kindly, shrewd face. Sure of Steve's interest, Al drew out a catalog and began to show him the new line of farm tools he was adding to his stock at the Tupper Hardware on Main Street.

Feeling Laurel's eyes upon him as he turned the pages, Stephen looked up and read her anxious speculation as to whether he would tell Al Tupper about the store in Willetts, North Dakota. He thought her slight frown and the tight line of her mouth meant, *Not yet,* and he nodded imperceptibly to show her that he understood perfectly. By ten-thirty, at the latest, he had figured, he would have to come out.

"Oh, say, folks!" exclaimed Al, his homely face contrite. "If I didn't forget to bring home those new electric lights for the tree! Had them all laid out on the counter. I'll just run down to the store and get them—only take a minute. Maybe Steve will go with me."

"Oh, no, don't, Al," said Laurel. "I'm glad you forgot them. We can use candles again. Here's a whole box. And here are the big ones to put in the windows."

"Yes, have everything the way Mother had it," urged Mr. Dean, leaning forward in his Morris chair by the secretary. "I've been wanting to tell you all something. You're making a great mistake to talk all around her the way you've been doing. When Helen said a nice, normal thing about Mother's dried beef gravy, she looked as if she'd made a break of some kind. You're running around here making a clatter to keep from thinking about her. That isn't right. Think about her! Talk about her! When you're old and alone, you'll know what I know: no one dies as long as love remembers."

There was a moment of silence, rich with recognition, in the Christmas-cluttered room. Laurel spoke first. Reaching out her hand to the brown wicker rocker and laying it like a caress on the folded white square, she said softly, "Mother's shawl. She left it there when she went into the other room."

"'The other room,'" said Mr. Dean eagerly. "That's how I think of it. Lollie, I remember when I bought that shawl for her—when Norman was a baby. She liked the feel of it about her shoulders—light, but warm. Last winter she got it out again and kept it on her chair."

"Norm! Do you see this gap in the fringe? That's where *you* hacked it out with the kitchen scissors, to make yourself a Rip Van Winkle beard."

"I ought to have been spanked all right, but what I remember is how mother laughed when she came to our show in the barn."

Helen, on her knees before the cardboard boxes, held up a shapeless bit of black flannel decorated with peanuts.

"The Peanut Man!" exclaimed Mr. Dean, taking it in his hand and turning it over thoughtfully. "When you were babies, Mrs. Parker, our next-door neighbor, made it for our tree. It was a Chinaman with a long queue down his back—quite a dignified fellow. On Christmas Eve the neighbors used to visit all the trees in the block and take some little thing for the trimming. It was a nice custom. Mother started it."

"See that scorched spot on his coat?" Norman pointed out. "Remember Mother's story about that? She said when a twig caught fire from a short candle, the Peanut Man swung and twisted on his cord until he broke it so that he could fall on the fire and put it out for us."

"And *you* said," Helen added, "'Huh, his string burned and he had to fall.' And then Mother said, 'Let's give him the benefit of the doubt. Always expect the best from everyone.'"

Mr. Dean showed Inga the gold star he held in his hand, then passed it up to Laurel, who had mounted the step ladder. "Here, Lollie, don't forget the star for the tip. Mother made it. She was always making pretty things."

"Didn't she used to paint a little, Father?"

"More than a little. She graduated from the Art School in Cincinnati, and opened a little studio of her own to give lessons. She had it only a year, because we were married then, and I wanted to go back West to take over the paper when it got too much for your grandfather."

"Why, she never told me that!" said Laurel. "I never dreamed she was professional."

"It must have slipped her mind. She was always pretty busy."

When the tree was decked to everyone's satisfaction, Stephen stole a look at his watch. It was past ten. Was Laurel leaving it to him after all? Still, there had been no suitable moment to broach the matter. He tried to catch her eyes, but she would not look his way. Into his anxiety and indecision came Helen's kind voice: "Poor Steve, we gabby Deans haven't given you a chance to get a word in edgewise. Tell us about some Christmas you remember."

Stephen could only stammer in confusion. "Well . . . you know I hadn't any real home. I remember—that time your mother asked me to spend my Christmas vacation here. The last night the tree was to be up—I remember—Lollie and I came in late from a party, and she lighted the candles for me once more, and somehow, there by the tree we knew . . . well, Christmas always means Lollie to me."

Appalled at his intimate revelation before them all, he broke off, half expecting to hear Laurel's "Don't be sentimental, Steve." But her face was turned away from him. There was something tense in the slant of her red-brown head. Maybe she'd like it if he left the room and gave her a clear field. He stood up decisively, saying with a brisk change of tone, "Guess I'll go out to the kitchen to have a visit with Grace. I hear her still thumping around out there, and I promised her I'd see if I could fix the ice-box leak. By the way, Helen, is she still engaged to her old faithful, the ice-man with the Chester A. Arthur whiskers?"

Helen laughed. "The status quo is unchanged. She'll neither set the day nor give him up altogether. She has a queer complex about divorce. Having read that every sixth marriage ends in divorce, she fears hers might be the inevitable sixth that goes on the rocks. As if it were a matter of statistics, and not clashing wills."

As Stephen went to the kitchen, Mr. Dean arose, absent-mindedly winding his watch. When Stephen came back, only Laurel was in the sitting room, moving restlessly about, stooping now and then to pick a bit of tinsel from the rug.

"They've all gone to bed to get some sleep before the children begin in the morning," she said, not looking at him.

"Oh! Well—then you'll have to make my goodbyes for me in the morning. What do you think old Grace said to me?"

"I haven't a notion."

"She's invited us—you and me—to come to her wedding New Year's Day. Her mind's made up at last. And by what? By observing the marital bliss of the Deans. She said, 'When I see how happy you all are, with every man for his wife, and every woman for her husband—and not even death big enough to separate you, I know I'm a timid old fool to miss out on four-teen years of lovin'.'"

"Don't laugh," said Laurel tensely. "It isn't funny."

"You must admit it has its humorous aspect. Though I grant you, in view of the situation, it has a certain element of pathos."

"Don't talk that silly, stilted way! I—I can't bear it."

Taut as a rubber binder stretched too thin, she reproached him: "Now I've got to take the brunt of it all alone—on Christmas morning."

"Oh! Then you didn't tell them? I understood you were going to find a time to break it gently."

"Then why did you make it impossible for me by telling that—about the tree and us? Oh, well, let it go. . . . Pete will be here for you any minute."

"Lollie," said Stephen gently, noting how white and strained she looked, "will you do something for me? Will you light the tree?"

"No," she said. "I—I won't."

With cool decision she put down the candle he held out to her.

At that Stephen's own nerves seemed to snap. "All right—all right," he heard himself biting off the words between his teeth. "I'm going to . . ." As he stepped toward her, she stepped back, furious at him. The sleeve of her sheer dress swung past the candle. There was a blaze, bright and terrible as the face of sudden death. Horror gripped Stephen, but love set him free to act swiftly. He leaped at the brown rocker, snatched the white wool shawl, wrapped her close. Tight against his breast he held her in an unbearable agony of fear and deep, protective passion. She trembled violently, and then, relaxing, began to sob in long, shuddering gasps of terror and release.

"Oh, Lollie, darling, darling," he besought her,

"forgive me! I was a beast to you! I'm afraid to look—to see whether you're horribly burned. . . ."

"No, Steve, no, I'm not—because you were so quick to save me. See, Steve, it's only a little red. Oh, Steve, Mother's shawl was there!"

"Where she left it for us, Lollie."

"It gives a lovely light," she repeated to herself.

"I don't understand. . . ."

"There's something about the shawl. Oh, I know I don't sound rational. But I am, really, Steve. I mean something about her life is still shining—a lovely light. I couldn't tell them about us, Steve, because I saw—I hoped—that our children would keep *me* living with the remembrance of little things."

His arms tightened about her, and, through tears, she smiled at him. Then, suddenly alert, she lifted her head from his shoulder and asked, "What time is it?"

"No matter. Just past eleven, I think."

"You'll miss the train. Why, Pete didn't come!"

"When I was in the kitchen, I phoned him not to. I'll wire in the morning that I've changed my mind. How can I go, Lollie?"

Laurel's still-wet eyes brightened with purpose. "Steve, that train waits a half hour in St. Paul. We can catch it, if we take the new cut-off. Quick, help me tie up my arm, and I'll change into a warm dress. This sleeve's a wreck."

"Lollie, you don't mean . . ."

"I'm going with you! Oh, Steve, I've tried so hard not to give in—to be a modern woman. Smart. Self-sufficient. But I can't be hard—because I've got a weak spot. For you, Steve. And I'm the one who's been a beast to you."

"I'm ashamed of that," he said contritely. . . .

Her arms tightened around him then, and her red-brown head rested on his shoulder again, close against his chin. "Just an old-fashioned wife who can't do without her husband."

"But the family, Lollie," Stephen suddenly remembered. "I can't take you away without a word like this. Perhaps you ought to come later. . . ."

"Please, Steve, right now. There's nothing like getting a good start on a new job. I can come back for a few days to close my studio. Grace is still up; she'll love to have news to tell in the morning. They'll understand. This is marriage, Steve, and we've—I've—never even tried it."

It had stopped snowing now, and a high moon, misted with a shining aureole, made glorious a new white world. Stephen pressed the starter. "Wait a minute," cried Laurel. "There's Grace on the porch, with her head all tied up. She's waving goodbye like mad. I forgot to wish her . . ."

She stepped down into a snowdrift and floundered back to the house. Impulsively she kissed the rough, cold cheek, wet with tears of true sentiment.

"I'm sorry we must miss your wedding, Grace, dear. All our best wishes for your happiness."

"And I'm tellin' you, Lollie, with your example plain before me as the nose on my face, I'd be a loony if I couldn't hit it off with Gus. You just back 'em up good, ain't that about the size of it?"

Laurel laughed. "It's the old reliable recipe, Grace. Goodbye! Happy days! And merry Christmas!"

Esther Chapman Robb

Esther Chapman Robb wrote for popular and inspirational magazines during the first half of the twentieth century.

Annie Hamilton Donnell

THE THIN LITTLE
LONELY ONE

Twelve-year-old Timothy had no one to love him, yet he had so much love locked inside him that yearned to be expressed. He decided to pour all that love into trimming the orphanage tree.

With unexpected results.

❄ ❄ ❄

Annie Hamilton Donnell's stories about mother love—though a century old—have been gathered to the heart by a new generation.

*I*t had never occurred to Timothy to boast that he had seen more Christmas trees than any other twelve-year-old boy in the country. For one thing, Timothy was not a boaster, and for another, the kind of Christmas trees that he had seen had looked very much like any other trees. They had not been Christmasy Christmas trees—no tinsel or glitter or color, and not a single present on them.

This year Timothy felt a good deal more than twelve years old. Importance oozed out of him, for he was to cut all the trees himself, undictated to and unwatched.

Mr. Stokes, the man Timothy lived with (and, incidentally, worked for), had broken his leg a week or two before tree-cutting time, and his rough wood was no place for a man on crutches. It was not to be thought of that the usual sale of Christmas trees be omitted. Simon Stokes never omitted a chance to make money. For years he had sent a certain number of shapely little trees to the nearest town to be trimmed and lighted and laden with gifts for little children, though the trimming and lighting and little children did not form any part of Simon Stokes' plans. He did not even know that a child lived with him. Timothy was only Timothy.

"Now, see you pick out a good one for the orphanage. They pay especial high for a good one, them ladies do. Last year's weren't big enough to suit 'em. There's a tree up other side o'—"

"I know! I know!" Timothy interrupted eagerly. Hadn't he already picked out the "Orphanage Tree"? For some reason that Timothy did not quite understand, the orphanage Christmas trees interested him most, and especially this year. Why, he really would be sending that tree to the orphans! He would pick it out and patiently hack at its trunk with his lean little arms, and bind its branches to its sides, and make a neat bundle of it—that was doing something toward sending a tree!

"I know exactly the one," Timothy said. "I know those rich ladies'll like that one—it's just as even-looking all round—when it's all trimmed up."

Timothy had a mental vision of the orphans' tree "all trimmed up." It was a beautiful vision, if a little unlike the reality, for Timothy had never seen an actual one. There were hundreds of little oil lamps lighting Timothy's vision-tree.

It was mid-December, but almost spring-mild. Or perhaps it was the warm little wave of excitement that made the day so comfortable to Timothy. He wore his raggedy old sweater unbuttoned, and even forgot the upper button of his flannel shirt.

"This is a nice day to cut Christmas trees," beamed Timothy. "I'll leave the Orphan Tree till last, so to have it to look forward to. I'll begin with just common Christmas trees."

Those were thrilling enough, but of course not to hold a candle—a Christmas tree candle—to the tree for little orphans.

In the night a clever idea had come to Timothy. It had grown and grown until now it was a big idea. He carried it about with him all the time he was selecting and sawing and binding up. Perhaps it was that idea that made Timothy so warm. Anyway, he hugged it up to him and kept getting better and better acquainted with it. By the time he got to the Orphan Tree how he liked that idea!

"I'll do it!" Timothy said aloud. Saying thoughts

aloud makes them kind of vows. The beautiful idea was to trim this tree he was going to send the orphans.

The Orphan Tree Timothy did not tie up into a big bundle, like the rest. Not yet—how could he until it was trimmed? He hurried back to the old farmhouse that he had called home for five years, ever since Simon Stokes had discovered working possibilities in the tiny boy's wiry little body and had offered to adopt him.

Up in the room under the eaves where the idea had been born, Timothy went to work on it. He got out his jackknife and bits of wood and sandpaper. Somewhere in the boy's active brain a wonder-working talent lay, and at its bidding Timothy, in his few leisure hours, whittled and sandpapered crude little works of art. Never mind what they might have been under more favorable circumstances, they were really remarkable little toys now. A set of doll's furniture was made and only needed to be packed. There was a tiny cradle, too, that a little unknown girl-orphan's doll could lie in. Timothy had spent a good deal of time making that diminutive cradle; its rockers were fastened cleverly to the bottom with wooden pegs of Timothy's own devising.

But those things were not enough to trim a tree. There must be one more, anyway, and Timothy decided it must be a very-little-child toy. He wanted an assortment of ages.

Bears—blacksmith bears—that was what! There was just time to make them if he hurried.

He had seen a toy like this once in the town in a special "Christmas display"; he knew how to make a better one! The bears should look like bears; they were to be arranged so that by pulling apart and pushing together two wooden levers they would beat upon a little wooden anvil with two tiny wooden hammers. Up and down—up and down—the blacksmith bears should pound industriously.

Timothy worked fast and eagerly. Little red happy spots blossomed out on his cheeks. He had never "trimmed" a tree before—it was great.

The three "trimmings" finished, and carefully wrapped up to make them mysterious, Timothy ticketed them. He cut out of a box cover three neat little cards and wrote on them: For the Thinnest One, For the Littlest One, For the Loneliest One.

The spelling was carefully correct. Timothy looked up "thinnest" in Mr. Stokes's ancient dictionary, to make sure of the right number of *n*s. The cradle was for the Thinnest One. The chairs and table looked sociable and the Loneliest One would like that. And of course, the Littlest One would like bears.

He took the toys down to the wood and fastened them securely in the undermost branches of the orphan tree, out of sight to casual notice. Then he bundled the tree and tied it. The two happy spots were still in his cheeks and two happy lights shone in his eyes. All around, under and over, were freckles and tough brown skin, but those little lights and spots made plain little Timothy handsome. For the first time in his twelve years of life he felt of importance in the world.

I hope the bears'll work all right, Timothy thought as he went back to the house. Oh, but they would—he knew those bears! The Littlest One would only have to do his part.

The trees were duly taken to the town and distributed. On the day before Christmas a number of ladies assembled in the committee room of the orphanage to trim the Christmas tree. How could they know it was already trimmed?

"It is a beauty this year!" Alicia Wellington exclaimed admiringly, as the shapely branches opened out. "Not much like last year's. I think the Lord planted this one for a little orphans' tree!"

"Speaking of orphans," one of the other ladies said, "when are you going to adopt one, as you once said you would, Alicia? You haven't given up the idea, have you?"

"Oh, no, don't give it up, Alicia! You would make such a darling mother," chimed in another voice. "You really must choose one." The voice had the sound of a mother in it. Alicia turned quickly.

"What do you know about choosing, Elinor West? Your little sons did not have to be chosen."

"No," laughed the voice, "I had to take them just as they were! Thomas Two now—I had to take him, little red head and all. Oh, Alicia," the mother-voice softened, "choose one, dear, choose one! You are losing so much. Come home with me tonight and watch Thomas Two hang up his stocking."

"Don't," interposed Alicia, "you hurt! I have never given it up, Elinor; but I haven't found him yet. Don't you see? I love every little one of them in this big house; but there isn't any of them the right one. I can't help believing I shall recognize mine."

"Perhaps," nodded Elinor. In her heart she was thanking the Lord that He had chosen hers for her.

The work of unpacking bundles and assorting gay

decorations preparatory to putting them in place on the tree went on rather silently. Then Alicia, who was bending the tree-branches back into position, uttered a soft little cry. She had discovered that the Orphan Tree was already trimmed. One at a time she read the dangling little cards.

"Oh!" softly cried Alicia. Her throat suddenly contracted and tears sprang to her eyes. She would not disclose her find to the others—not for a minute. She wanted those little cards to herself. She knew—she knew! Some inner mother voice told her that a thin little lonely one had written those cards. She read it—in the painful, cramped little words.

Very gently, all by herself, she unwrapped the three bundles and studied the cleverly constructed contents. A child had made them, and a child who was little and lonely and thin. Alicia gazed through her tears, a throbbing ache in her heart. What had happened to her? Had she found hers?

"See," she said quietly, a moment later, "see what I have found, will you? Someone has sent three little orphans a present. The dearest little things! I mean to find out who it was."

The others examined and admired. The mother-one thrilled—"Why," she said, "the trees come from the same place every year. It ought to be easy to find out where from. Ask the superintendent, Alicia. I'm sure somebody said the trees were brought to town in a wagon, so it can't be very far—where's Alicia? I'm talking to her!"

Alicia had already gone to find the superintendent. He was not in his office and she had to wait. Waiting was not easy to Alicia. She went back reluctantly to join the other women. All the morning her mind dwelt on the "Thin Little Lonely One"! Could it be she had created him entirely out of her own fancy? No—no—somewhere she would find him!

"If it was a child that made those darling little toys, and Alicia's sure it is, then he ought to come to this tree," Elinor West declared with emphasis. "We must find out somehow before tonight. If you could go in your car, Alicia—you haven't any little stockings to hang up. I mean go wherever the superintendent says the tree came from, and see if it was a child—"

"I know, I am going," Alicia said quietly. She and her swift car would find that Thin Little Lonely One in time.

The superintendent himself did not know, but he made inquiries. Simon Stokes's farm was the place, ten miles out. He was the man that had supplied their Christmas tree every year for nobody knew how long.

To the farm of Simon Stokes went Alicia in her car. She was curiously impatient. What was she to find? All the way she fluttered her hands nervously. Alicia the calm—excited!

It was Timothy who answered her knock on the weather-worn old front door—thin and little and lonely-looking Timothy! She recognized him at once. When she had made known her errand and, astonished and thrilled, little Timothy had hurried away to put on his best clothes for the orphans' tree, Alicia turned to Simon Stokes.

"Are you his—does he belong to you?" she asked. But she knew she had read in Timothy's face that he did not belong.

"If anyone—if I should find a home for him, where he

could be sure of—of love and of being educated—you would not make any objection, would you, Mr. Stokes?"

It was Christmas time o' year—was that why Simon Stokes answered he would not stand in the boy's way? Let her find the boy that kind of a home if she could—Timothy was a good boy—mebbe he'd ought to have a better chance—mebbe 'twas only right.

So it came about that for the first time the boy who had seen so many Christmas trees saw a Christmasy one, aglow with color and lights and gifts. And he had gifts, too. His empty little cup suddenly ran over. But something bigger was hung on the Orphan Tree for this Thin Little Lonely One—a home and mother-love.

Annie Hamilton Donnell
(1862–?)

Annie Hamilton Donnell, late in the nineteenth century and early in the twentieth, was one of the most beloved family writers in America. Her favorite subject was motherhood and children. Besides writing prolifically for family magazines, she also wrote books such as *Rebecca Mary* (1905), *The Very Small Person* (1906), and *Miss Theodosia's Heartstrings* (1916).

Denise A. Boiko

JEANETTE'S
CHRISTMAS LIST

Company was coming for Christmas, and Jeanette wanted everything to be just right. So—as she always did—she made a list. And—as she always did—she kept adding to it.

Then came the phone call. . . .

*C*learing a space on her cluttered dining-room table, Jeanette sat down with a blank spiral notebook and a sharp pencil in her hands and a determined look on her face. The determination was swiftly replaced by frustration as, one by one, three shrieking, dark-haired whirlwinds careened past her, grasping her chair on their circuit around the table.

"Kids, please try not to disturb me," Jeanette urged. "I'm making my Christmas list."

The tallest of the whirlwinds halted with a look of interest on her face.

"You mean a list of what you want for Christmas?"

"No, a list of what I want to get *done* before Christmas. It's already the sixteenth of December. School lets out this Friday for Christmas vacation, and I haven't done half the things I need to do before the grandmas and grandpas and Aunt Tricia and Uncle David come for Christmas."

The middle whirlwind, a lad of perhaps six, tugged at his older sister's arm, eager to resume the chase. The smallest, a dimpled cherub of about four, tried to climb up onto her mother's lap.

Jeanette sighed.

"Sarah, it would be a huge help to me if you'd take Tyler and April into another room and start a game. A quiet game. Or if that's too much to ask, maybe a video."

"Okay, Mommy. Good luck with your list. Maybe I'll make one too."

Jeanette had to smile. She herself was notorious for drawing up lengthy lists for every occasion, and Sarah, her third-grader, already showed signs of being a "planner" too. Whenever her husband, Curtis, came across the scraps of paper on which Sarah's lists were recorded, he smacked his forehead and lamented, "Oh, no! She's inherited the list-making gene!"

Taking a deep breath as the giggling trio charged out of the room, Jeanette returned to her list. Her brow furrowed as she wrote:

1. Plan menu.
2. Try different dessert recipes and decide on one.
3. Make a Christmas centerpiece for the table.

Pausing for a moment, Jeanette picked up a magazine which had several pages marked. She studied a photo of a stunning centerpiece using metallic gold candles, ribbon, and shiny Christmas balls. Or maybe she'd try the one with glass bowls of vanilla-scented candles and fresh cranberries. The same magazine featured at least a dozen recipes for pies, cookies, and other delicious desserts to cap off the perfect Christmas dinner. Setting the magazine aside, Jeanette continued writing.

4. Make new place mats, napkins, and table runner.

At this, Jeanette frowned. This would be a challenge, but she was skillful at sewing and thought she could manage it. To spruce up her aging ivory tablecloth, she had bought yards and yards of the perfect fabric—on clearance! Elegant and Christmasy, it was a deep maroon with textured threads of sparkly gold running through it. She had even purchased a bolt of clearance gold trim to accent it.

Adding number five to her list, she wrote:

5. Find Tyler something halfway decent to wear to church on Christmas Eve.
6. Shop for a Christmas dress for Sarah, too.

"April can wear one of Sarah's old dresses I've got tucked away," she mused. "But Tyler will be a complete ragamuffin unless I get busy and find him something." Her kindergartner was all boy and seemed to spend most of his waking hours on his knees and elbows.

Skipping into the room, Sarah announced, "I got Tyler and April settled for you, Mom. They're watching that new Christmas video we checked out from the church library." Stopping to peer over her mother's shoulder, she commented, "Nice list, Mom."

"Thanks so much, honey," Jeanette replied absently, before glancing at her daughter and adding:

7. Cut Sarah's hair, or at least her bangs.
8. Buy and wrap presents for the adults. *(Thankfully, she had finished shopping for the children.)*
9. Clean house thoroughly.
10. Bake Christmas cookies with kids.
11. Finish Christmas cards.

Jeanette examined her list critically. She might add a few items later, but this would do for a start. In fact—

As she recorded the numeral twelve to list one more task, the phone rang. Sighing, she picked up her cordless from where it sat on the dining-room table and answered, "Hello?"

"Mrs. Sheldon?"

"Yes?" Jeanette replied, her pencil still poised to record her twelfth task.

"This is Dr. Kingston. I need to tell you that we found a possible abnormality in your mammogram from last week. We'd like you to come in for another mammogram and some additional testing."

For a long moment, Jeanette could neither speak nor think. At last she found her voice.

"Does it look like cancer?" she asked quietly.

Dr. Kingston's voice was gentle. "We can't tell for sure yet, but please try not to get alarmed at this point. It could be anything . . . or nothing. However, given your family history, I'm going to recommend that we set up a biopsy appointment for you in case we discover that you need one. Since these appointments fill up quickly, I'm arranging to hold an appointment for you this Friday, December 20. If, after the repeat mammogram and other tests, we decide that you don't need the biopsy, we'll cancel that appointment. Meanwhile, can you come in for a mammogram tomorrow morning?"

Jeanette's mind was whirling. "Yes . . . yes, of course. I'll be there. What time should I come?"

"How about 9:30?"

"Okay, Dr. Kingston. Thank you for letting me know."

Jeanette hung up the phone slowly. Painfully. She was remembering her mother, who had died of breast cancer when Jeanette was in high school. Though her father had remarried several years later, and their family circle was once again warm and cheerful, Jeanette still thought about her mother every day. As a precaution, Jeanette had begun scheduling regular mammograms at a young age, but she had never dreamed that this first alarm would come at age thirty-five.

Anxiously she picked up her pencil and filled in number twelve on her list:

12. Arrange babysitters for tomorrow and Friday.

With a sigh, she added:

13. Pray.

Underlining her last item, she picked up the phone to call her husband.

❄ ❄ ❄

Tuesday and Wednesday passed quickly. After the second mammogram and an ultrasound test, Jeanette's doctor was still not satisfied with the looks of the suspicious area and instructed Jeanette to keep Friday's biopsy appointment.

By Wednesday afternoon, Jeanette was struggling with a growing anxiety about what Friday's procedure might reveal. To distract herself, she returned to her Christmas list to see what she could check off. While waiting at doctors' offices, she had finished her Christmas cards. Now she absentmindedly thumbed through cookbooks and magazines, looking at recipes for chocolate-caramel tortes and broccoli-cheese casseroles, as well as at photos of elaborate centerpiece creations. At the same time, she wondered whether she was up to hosting the family for Christmas this year. Yet she could not see any way out of it. Her sister and brother-in-law, with their two young boys, were joining them from out of town, as were Curtis's parents. Although her own father and stepmother lived nearby and would be willing to host the group if asked, it would be a tight squeeze in their tiny apartment. Moreover, she and Curtis had agreed not to mention this possible health crisis to the family until they knew something definite. Jeanette hated to cast a shadow on everyone's Christmas—especially her father's and sister's.

No, she would go through with the holiday as planned. If she scheduled the next few days carefully, it would all work out. Best of all, it would keep her mind off her worry. She should start her sewing project today and also make a shopping list. Tomorrow she could shop for the nonperishable groceries, buy outfits for Sarah and Tyler, and pick up materials for the centerpiece.

School was out for the afternoon, and Sarah had been busy in her room for the past hour. Now she appeared at Jeanette's side, beaming.

"Mommy, do you remember a few weeks ago when you said that because we're having company this Christmas we could put on a little Christmas show for them?"

Jeanette's heart sank.

"Uh . . . did I say that?"

"Yes, Mommy, remember? And that Christmas video gave me just the perfect idea! Me, Tyler, and April can be the three wise men bringing gifts to Baby Jesus. And we can all sing 'We Three Kings.'"

Hastily, Jeanette considered the idea. It would mean adding a few tasks to her list. But she *had* promised.

"Well, sure, honey, I guess we can do that."

"And I even made a list, Mommy, just like yours. I have it all planned out. See?"

Sarah thrust a smudged, much-erased piece of note-book paper in front of her mother. Jeanette read,

SARAH'S CHRISTMAS LIST
1. Baby Jesus (Aprils Dolly)
2. We 3 Kings (Us Kids)
3. Oddyents (Grandmas, Grandpas, ant, uncle, cuzzins)
4. Chairs
5. Papers
6. Tickets
7. Songs
8. Happy Birthday Jesus
9. Costumes
10. Gold
11. Frank and Sense
12. Murr

Jeanette smiled at some of the creative spelling. "OK, let's go over this. What do you mean by 'papers'?"

"Oh, those little sheets you give your audience that tell about the show."

"You mean programs?"

"Yes! We need programs."

Tapping her pencil on the table thoughtfully, Jeanette asked, "Do you think you can take care of the programs, tickets, and chairs yourself?"

"I can, Mommy. I'll start making the tickets today."

Jeanette took a deep breath as she reread the "costumes" item.

"What did you have in mind for costumes?"

"You know, long, pretty robes like the wise men had, with fancy things on our heads. Some sparkly stuff, too. Oh, it will be so much fun, Mommy! I already told April and Tyler, and they want to do it."

Putting her arm around her daughter, Jeanette said gently, "Honey, I don't know whether I can make fancy costumes in such a short time. Couldn't we do without?"

Sarah's eyes grew moist, and her voice quivered. "But then we wouldn't be the three kings, just three kids. Please, Mommy? I promise I'll help."

Jeanette took another deep breath and stood up. Striding purposefully toward her sewing closet, she pulled out the yards and yards of maroon and gold fabric she'd bought for the place mats and napkins.

"You're in luck, my dear. I have just the thing for the costumes."

Sarah squealed and ran her fingers over the elegant fabric. Jeanette returned to her own list, crossed out number four, "Make new place mats," and in its place wrote "Make wise men costumes." Then at the bottom of the list she added:

14. Find gold, frankincense, and myrrh.

❄ ❄ ❄

Thursday became a sewing day instead of a shopping day. While Tyler and Sarah were at school, Jeanette experimented with April. Asking her to lie down on a doubled length of the fabric, she had her spread her arms out as if making a snow angel. Carefully she traced an outline of her daughter's wiggling body and arms, leaving a few generous inches to spare around the edges and drawing a full skirt shape along April's legs. When she was finished being traced, April jumped up and watched her mother cut the fabric along the lines, make a six-inch slit down the middle of the back, and rapidly sew the two pieces together, leaving an opening for April's head. Jeanette finished it off by hemming the sleeves, neckline, and bottom edge of the gown. As she hemmed, she also attached a strip of gold braid to each edge. A snap closure at the back completed the costume, and it was time for a fitting.

April skipped around the room, exclaiming, "I'm a wise man!" When Jeanette picked Tyler up from kindergarten at noon, April was still wearing her costume. Tyler wanted one, too.

His was almost finished by the time Jeanette picked Sarah up at two o'clock. By dinnertime (which featured boxed macaroni-and-cheese and applesauce), all three costumes were ready, complete with fancy gold sashes and customized headdresses. Jeanette felt particularly proud of those. For April's and Sarah's, she had braided three long twisted strips of the maroon fabric and pinned the two ends together to form a simple head-piece. As she braided, she had worked in sparkly strips of metallic gold trim, and the effect was quite rich-looking. For Tyler, she had constructed a crown out of foil-covered cardboard. A few fake jewels from Sarah's toy jewelry kit provided the finishing touches.

The children danced around the dinner table, showing off their finery to their father. "We three kings of Orient are!" Sarah sang.

"Indeed you are," he agreed, smiling as they frolicked away into the next room. With a more serious look, he glanced at his wife. "Sarah told me about the play. Are you sure you're up to all this?"

Jeanette nodded, a lump suddenly coming to the back of her throat.

"I asked myself the same question today. In fact, as I sat there sewing at sixty miles per hour, I thought, *Why am I doing this?* At first I thought I was just keeping busy so I wouldn't worry so much. But then the answer came to me all of a sudden. What else *should* I be doing? Should I be out shopping for things we don't need, or spending the day decorating the house with trinkets that will be forgotten in two weeks? Or instead, shouldn't I be doing something with my kids that will help them worship Jesus and give them a memory they'll never forget?"

Jeanette paused, and tears came to her eyes. "Especially if . . . I'm not feeling well next Christmas or . . . I can't do it then." She took a deep breath. "I'm so worried about that biopsy tomorrow."

Curtis gripped her hand across the dinner table. "We'll try not to worry about that right now, honey." He sighed too, but then smiled warmly at her. "I do believe this will be a Christmas we'll remember for years to come."

The biopsy was scheduled for Friday morning. Curtis accompanied Jeanette to the surgery center after dropping Sarah and Tyler at school and leaving April with Jeanette's best friend, Kim, with whom they had shared what was going on. The procedure was finished more quickly than Jeanette had expected. Before noon, they were on their way home with instructions that they'd hear the results in about a week.

Though the biopsy had been performed under a local anesthetic, the emotions of the week had left Jeanette drained. By the time they arrived home, all she wanted to do was to crawl into bed. She napped while Curtis picked up April and Tyler and made lunch. As she slept, she found herself dwelling on images of three little wise men bearing gold, frankincense, and myrrh. Despite the anxiety that kept pushing its way to the surface, Jeanette knew one thing for certain. It was more important than ever to focus on Christ this Christmas.

Waking up in the late afternoon, still a little groggy, Jeanette wandered into the kitchen and pulled out her Christmas list. Curtis was starting dinner, and the aroma of browning hamburger and onions filled the kitchen. Sarah sat at the table painstakingly making programs and tickets.

Bless her heart, Jeanette thought to herself. *This means so much to her.* Glancing at the sheet of paper Sarah was working with, Jeanette asked, "Where did you get that fancy lettering?"

"Daddy did it on the computer." Sarah beamed as she showed her mother the front cover. Adorned with a colorful cutout of the wise men from an old Christmas card, it read, "We Three Kings Christmas Show." Inside was printed the Scripture passage from the book of Matthew, telling the story of the visit of the wise men.

"Our names are in there!" Tyler pointed out.

"And the words to the song, too," Sarah indicated. "I'm making the tickets, because everyone needs a ticket. Tyler's going to sell tickets, but really they're free. And

April is going to hand out programs. They're free too. It's all free. And I'm going to be the announcer."

"You've planned this well," Jeanette commented, sitting down at the table. "I'm impressed."

"Did you have a good nap, Mommy?" April asked, crawling into her lap.

"I sure did, sweetie. What a nice Daddy you have, to make lunch and dinner."

"Spaghetti and meatballs!" Curtis announced. "It won't be ready for a while, though. Oh, by the way—Kim wanted me to give you this bag. Some clothes her kids have outgrown."

"Oh—let me see." Jeanette opened the bag to find a pair of dark gray slacks and a festive red sweater in Tyler's size. Underneath it was a green plaid dress with a black velvet collar and a white bow at the neck.

At the bottom of the bag was a note from Kim.

> Hi, Jeanette—
> Chase has outgrown this sweater and the pants, and I thought they might fit Tyler. This new dress is a gift for Sarah. My Nicole has one just like it and begged me to let her be "twins" with Sarah. Maybe she can wear it to church Christmas Eve. But no hard feelings if you already have another dress in mind. I love you and I'm praying for you.
> Kim

Jeanette's eyes glistened with tears. With gratitude, she took a pen and crossed out items five and six on her list. "Thank you, Lord," she whispered.

On Saturday Jeanette rummaged through her Christmas CDs until she found the music to "We Three Kings." Now almost as enthusiastic as Sarah, she worked with the kids until they could sing the chorus accurately, loudly, and nearly on key. Sarah could also read the words to the verses, and Tyler knew some of them, as well. Next, Jeanette launched a search for gold, frankincense, and myrrh. For frankincense, she found an ornate turquoise-and-gold cookie tin with a fancy lid. For myrrh, she produced a small, Middle-Eastern-looking vase. Filling it with spicy potpourri, she stuffed the opening with a ball of aluminum foil as a stopper. Now all that was left was gold.

"OK, kids, help me find some gold," she called.

"I got some, Mommy!" Tyler yelled, tugging at a long string of beaded garland on the Christmas tree.

"Whoa, there, honey! Let me help." Jeanette intervened just in time to prevent the tree from toppling over. Removing the glittering gold garland, she handed it to Tyler.

As he reverently passed the garland from one hand to another, Jeanette had the distinct impression that he believed he was holding pure gold.

"Can I be the disciple with gold?" he pleaded.

"Sure, Tyler. Only I think you mean *wise man*, not *disciple.*"

"And I'm frankincense and April is myrrh!" Sarah exclaimed.

Sarah wrapped Baby Jesus (April's most lifelike doll) in swaddling clothes (a strip of fabric confiscated from Jeanette's sewing closet) and placed Him in April's doll cradle.

"There's Baby Jesus," she announced proudly. "Let's practice giving Him our gifts."

As if on cue, they all knelt and held out their gifts.

"This is going to be a great show!" Sarah exclaimed.

❋ ❋ ❋

The weekend passed quickly. On Monday, Kim offered to watch the three children while Jeanette slipped out to finish her Christmas shopping. Whatever grand ideas Jeanette had entertained regarding gifts for the grandparents and her sister's family, they were now dismissed in favor of the practical and time-saving.

"I guess gift certificates will have to do," Jeanette concluded.

With three or four quick stops at favorite stores and restaurants, she was finished.

But when she arrived home to proudly cross item eight off her list, she was horrified to discover item number one confronting her boldly. She hadn't done a thing about planning Christmas dinner! Jeanette, the quintessential organizer, had slipped up. Today was Monday. Christmas was Wednesday. That wasn't even enough time to thaw a turkey.

"Don't panic," she consoled herself. "What is *really* important here?"

Suddenly a calm feeling came over her. Picking up the phone, she dialed her supermarket and placed an order for a precooked Christmas dinner. She chose the baked ham dinner with all the trimmings: sauce, dinner rolls, and extra orders of scalloped potatoes and green bean casserole. She could fill in with a salad or two, and her stepmother would be bringing her famous sweet potato casserole.

"I've always wanted to try one of those dinners, anyway," she rationalized.

Things were falling into place. What was left? Well, there was dessert. The dinner came with one pie, but that wouldn't be enough for thirteen people. Although she could easily pick up another pie, it would be nice to have some variety.

April came and snuggled into her lap.

"I been thinkin', Mama," she announced, stroking Jeanette's cheek.

"What have you been thinkin', darlin'?" Jeanette asked, burying her face in April's glossy dark hair, which smelled sweetly of baby shampoo. What a precious child! How she wanted to be here, for many Christmases to come, with her beloved four-year-old—with all of them, and with Curtis, and with the whole family.

Swallowing the lump in her throat, she turned her attention back to April.

"When do we make the Happy Birthday Jesus cake, Mama?"

Jeanette gasped quietly. Their yearly tradition—and somehow she'd forgotten this, too!

"The Happy Birthday Jesus cake! Thank you so *much* for reminding me, sugarplum. Let's see. Tomorrow is Christmas Eve. Why don't we bake it tomorrow when the grandmas and grandpas get here, and then that can be our special dessert for Christmas dinner the next day? What kind do you think we should make?"

April took her time pondering this serious decision. At last, with big eyes and a thoughtful look, she asked,

"Do you think Jesus likes chocolate cake with chocolate frosting and sprinkles?"

Jeanette smiled, giving her daughter an extra-long hug.

"Honey, I think that's His very favorite."

April ran off joyfully.

That left Christmas cookies to bake. Since this was another Sheldon family tradition, she was surprised that none of the children had asked about them yet. They loved spreading icing and colored sprinkles on festive Christmas shapes.

"Maybe we could do that this afternoon right after lunch," Jeanette mused. "But this calls for another shortcut."

Rounding up the kids for a quick trip to the store, she bought colored sprinkles, canned vanilla icing, and several packages of ready-to-roll sugar cookie dough. In just half an hour, the kitchen was filled with the fragrance of warm cookies as the first batch came out of the oven. After setting up decorating stations for the kids, Jeanette almost smugly crossed number two and number ten off her list. With a smile, she also crossed off number seven, Sarah's haircut. There wasn't time, and it really didn't matter.

Glancing at number three, she thought aloud. "I meant to make a special centerpiece for the table. Well, maybe I'll think of something before Christmas Day."

Cleaning the house *thoroughly* was number nine on the list. Jeanette just had to laugh at that one. She crossed out *thoroughly* and wrote *lightly*. Looking at it for a moment longer, she crossed out the whole line and shrugged her shoulders, which suddenly felt as though a burden had been lifted from them. In a year of life-and-death priorities, cleaning house just didn't make it to the top of the list.

On December 24, Curtis's parents arrived in the late morning, and Jeanette's father and stepmother stopped by two hours later to help with the day's festivities. The three children immediately sequestered their grandmothers in the kitchen to make the Happy Birthday Jesus cake. After an hour, the children emerged, displaying various degrees of chocolate face.

Curtis came home from work early, and Jeanette's sister and brother-in-law, with their two sons, Andrew and Justin, arrived at about the same time. After a Chinese take-out dinner and a few quick baths and showers, everyone headed off to church in his or her best Christmas finery.

Never had the Christmas carols meant more to Jeanette; never had her heart felt more full than it did on this Christmas Eve. Gazing at the candlelit sanctuary and inhaling the fragrance of candles and fresh pine Christmas trees, she contemplated all that was being celebrated tonight. As they sang "O Little Town of Bethlehem," she fully understood the line "the hopes and fears of all the years are met in Thee tonight." Jeanette certainly carried her share of hopes and fears tonight. During the dark Christmasy hush of "Silent Night," she wiped away tear after tear, unable to keep from wondering what next Christmas would hold for her family. Praying fervently, she clutched Curtis's hand, and he squeezed hers in understanding.

After church, the evening continued with Christmas music, cookies, hot chocolate, and conversation. Just before bedtime the family gathered for devotions around the Advent wreath. As Curtis lit the Christ candle in the center of the wreath, Jeanette thought, as she did every year, that nothing could be more beautiful or more symbolic of Christmas.

❄ ❄ ❄

Christmas morning passed in a flurry of stockings, gifts, breakfast, laughter, and phone calls to other relatives.

As she heated up her prepackaged dinner, deftly disposing of the telltale boxes, she set the table, carefully and lovingly. Oh dear! She'd forgotten about the centerpiece. But somehow, ribbon, metallic candles, and gold balls no longer held any appeal for her. When she spotted the Advent wreath in the living room, she realized that nothing could be more worthy of adorning the table at Christmas. Placing it reverently on the table, she whispered, "Thank you for being the Light of the World."

The glow of candlelight from the Advent wreath illuminated a Christmas dinner filled with conversation, reminiscing, and compliments.

"Great meal, Jeanette," her brother-in-law, David, commented. "This sauce for the ham is incredible. You'll have to give Tricia your recipe."

Jeanette thanked him with a smile, giving a sly wink to Curtis's mother, who had caught her disposing of the large carton the dinner came in.

After the meal, Jeanette announced, "Before dessert, we have a little surprise for all of you. We're proud to present the Sheldon children in 'We Three Kings'!"

The kids bustled about, setting up chairs in the living room. Tyler "sold" tickets while April handed out programs. With this bit of business finished, they ran off to change into their costumes. Jeanette prepared the CD player and hastened to assist the wise men with their headpieces. Curtis moved the Advent wreath to a prominent place and lit it again. Placing the doll cradle squarely in the middle of the room, he picked up his Bible and awaited his signal from Director Sarah.

When she peeked her elegant head around the corner and whispered "Now!" Curtis began reading the Scripture passage. As he came to the conclusion, "they opened their treasures and presented Him with gifts of gold and of incense and myrrh," Jeanette started the music. The children marched in solemnly to the opening chords of "We Three Kings."

"Everyone in the audience sing," Sarah prompted. "The words are in your papers." So everyone sang, and at the appropriate verse, each little wise man lovingly presented his or her gift to Baby Jesus.

Jeanette then switched the CD to the "Hallelujah Chorus," and the three wise men held their gifts up reverently over the cradle.

Midway through the music, April suddenly dropped her jar of myrrh and picked up Baby Jesus. "Don't, April! That's not how it goes!" whispered Sarah indignantly.

But April was oblivious to her sister's directions. Hugging and kissing the doll, with its makeshift swaddling clothes dangling half off its little body, she held that pose until the end of the music.

It was a moment Jeanette wanted to picture forever— Sarah, with her bangs in her eyes, gazing lovingly at the baby, April holding it close, and Tyler draping his precious strands of gold over the baby's feet. As the music faded and the audience clapped, Jeanette found herself thinking, *I'm so glad I made time for this. I wouldn't have missed it for anything! And it's all free, just as Sarah said.*

"Time for the birthday party!" April exclaimed, carrying Baby Jesus to the table and seating Him prominently next to her.

"Jeanette, what a great Christmas this has been," her stepmother remarked as Jeanette lit the birthday candles. "Knowing you and your lists, I'm sure you've been planning it for weeks!"

Jeanette smiled, realizing that this Christmas had come about *in spite of,* not because of, her lists. In the glow of candlelight on the chocolate birthday cake, her children's faces beamed as they sang "Happy Birthday, dear Jesus!" She had never felt more joyful.

When her doctor telephoned two days later to report that her biopsy was completely normal, Jeanette's heart rejoiced again. But somehow, she knew that she had already received the best gift on Christmas night.

Denise A. Boiko

Denise A. Boiko is a contemporary freelance writer, writing from her home in San Jose, California.

Dorothea Allen McKemie

MEMORIES OF
A GOLDEN NIGHT

It was Christmas—but affluence was gradually destroying it. They were less and less together, and the gap between them widened with each passing year.

So, she figured, what can I lose by going back to when we had nothing?

❄ ❄ ❄

This story has been in the running for many years now—it is time.

*A*ll the gifts had been opened. Bright papers, crumpled ribbons, bows, boxes, tags, and her two grandchildren littered the floor of the sun porch, and the aroma of turkey and sage was lightly layered above them. This Christmas had been a chore for him, she knew. What was there left to give a wife whose eyes showed a hunger, yet who had every *thing,* a wife who surely needed nothing more?

In years past, in the years of their striving together, the "thin years" he liked to call them now, he had chosen wisely some needed gift that often pleased and always surprised. He would wrap it himself, clumsily, and then write enigmatic clues to its contents on a used Christmas card he taped to the package. On those Christmases past he often withheld that gift until the last, after she had examined the presents under the tree every day. Then, on Christmas morning, when all other presents had been discovered and unwrapped and admired, he would make his offering to her, wrapped in last year's paper, last year's ribbon not quite covering last year's crease, last year's Christmas card taped crookedly on top, endearing him and his package to her in a wave of color and affection.

But now, now that affluence had come to dwell among them, his gifts to her came in small, sleek jeweler's boxes or towering packages from Neiman Marcus. Last year's gift had been a southern cruise for two, but a daughter had accompanied her, the press of business keeping him at home. This arrangement had pleased neither of them, she knew, but ease will exact its payment, so that now they often traveled separate ways, nodding congenially as their orbits crossed, her growing hunger unrelieved, his unknown and unreckoned.

·This year, it lay on the table beside her African violet, his gift to her. It had been an ounce of "Joy" perfume and a cruise brochure featuring a Far Eastern tour on the *Queen Elizabeth II*.

"For yourself and companion," his card had read. They no longer dealt in the foolish conventions of "you and I."

Last Christmas she had given him a gold watch, an imported cashmere sweater set that proved too warm for Texas winters, and a golden pen tucked in his Christmas stocking hung by the fireplace. This year's Christmas shopping had begun in the usual way. But midway, while buying a board game for her eldest grandchild (a game of chance, of throw the dice and win a fortune, draw a card and become famous, spin the wheel and lose your job) a wild memory had seized her. When she came home that day she stored the presents she had already bought for his Christmas and substituted a single gift which she had bought for him at a drugstore in the mall.

For days before, and especially this morning during the frenzy of gift-giving, she had been aware of the wonder in his eyes—that there was no present for him, from her, among all the others. When she saw him poke a toe at the jumble of wrappings at his feet, she stood up, stepped over the litter and the grandchildren, and went to the pantry, returning to stand over him, offering a package crudely wrapped in last year's paper. There were no words written across the Christmas card she had taped to the top. Last year's ribbon did not quite cover last year's crease. She sat down opposite him as he weighed her offering with hands and eyes. He looked at

her once, an unquestioning look. His eyes, behind
trifocal glasses framed in gold, met hers appraisingly, as if
he dared not hope. When her daughters began their
questions, she silenced them sharply with a look and
turned to give her attention to him.

Beneath the wrappings his fingers felt and recognized
the outline of a box, and at once he *knew*. Then remi-
niscence came to sit silently beside them both, like an
old friend telling all with a touch so that, remembering,
they traveled backward in time together.

They had been married only a few months that Christmas of 1945, and it was to have been an adventurous
holiday for her, filled with new family and new friends
and a taste of the soon-to-be new life in Texas. They
had been camping in a dark and drafty brownstone near
the campus in south Chicago, he finishing his studies
toward his degree, she daily dusting soot from
windowsills, pulling the Murphy bed up and down,
washing clothes in the bathtub and ironing them on the
kitchen table. Waiting. Waiting for the new life in
Texas to begin.

His parents had paid for train tickets to bring them to
Texas for the holidays and had planned a gathering of
friends and relatives to meet her. She was only reason-
ably apprehensive. For the occasion she made a lovely
dress of blue, with a long skirt and puffed sleeves and
bugle beads at the neck. She would wear her hair
upswept, with a flower tucked under the curls on top.

She shopped carefully for his family's Christmas gifts,

and considering the small amount of money allowable for presents, and the fact that she had not yet met his younger sister, she was fairly pleased with her selections. These gifts, the new dress, their small gifts to each other, and most of the rest of their clothing she had packed in a footlocker and sent on ahead to Texas six days earlier. In those days baggage transit was a chancy thing, since trains were crowded with the materials of the aftermath of war.

❄ ❄ ❄

Now she stood with him, their bodies pressed closely side by side, swaying and shuddering in the immense crowd of people that packed the concourse of the railway station in downtown Chicago. The war had ended four months before and now thousands who had been displaced by it had begun to seek their rightful places, coming together in airports and depots, in cab and bus and subway traffic, mixing and swirling like debris caught in a swollen stream that seeks its level. She and the boy who held her tight bobbed in the backwaters of the old Illinois Central station. The enormity of this crowd was surprising—and terrifying. An army of travelers surrounded them.

The heat, the mingled smells of leather and oil and sweat, were all the more oppressive in the din of noises that reverberated through the cavernous old station. The shuffle of thousands of feet across its marble floors, the fragmented conversations of the weary, the cries of babies, the yelps of tired children, the boom of the public address system, the coughing, hacking, racking noises of frustration and aggravation and fear, all fumed and roiled and boiled together with the smoke of bodies, of steam heat and tobacco, to form a great cloud of lamentation that floated to the top of the vaulted ceiling.

Men, women, children all slowly pushing on toward the iron departure gates, carrying her and her husband forward inch by inch. Elbows, duffels, and suitcases jabbed their bodies, babies cried and fell into exhausted sleep, a woman near them fainted and remained upright, so tightly packed was the crowd. She began to feel faint traces of a giggle that came unannounced and was soon to churn up her innards in its bid for freedom. She recognized fear and panic in it, and he held her closer and kissed her hair.

❄ ❄ ❄

When the time had come and gone for the departure of their train, and they were still trapped far back in the crowd, he held her in his arms as everyone pushed past.

"Don't cry," he told her, kissing her lightly. "We'll have our own Christmas, here in Chicago . . . just the two of us."

The footlocker, filled with most of their clothes and all of their Christmas, had already reached Texas without them as on Christmas Eve they walked to the shops on Sixty-Third Street in south Chicago. At a drugstore they bought a one-pound box of Sampler candy for the landlady who had invited them to share her Christmas dinner. Then they each took two dollars and parted, under the elevated tracks, to make a Christmas for themselves.

She shopped wisely, buying him a new hairbrush, a pair

of argyle socks, a new razor, and two packages of blades. She knew that two dollars would buy any number of wonderful things for her: a pair of rhinestone earrings, a silk scarf, the latest Wodehouse, a big bottle of eau de cologne. Instead, he bought a small wisp of a Christmas tree with needles falling, and something wrapped in a drugstore bag. Because when the Murphy bed came down, there was no space in their one room for a tree, he hung it in a corner from a bent nail in the ceiling. Through the window the gray glow of a streetlight softened its peculiar list.

❊ ❊ ❊

Toward midnight, in their Murphy bed, sipping coffee and listening to the needles drop, he unwrapped his presents and was pleased. He brushed his hair and put on his new socks (they looked well with his pajamas) and put the razor and blades aside for use later. Then he handed her the drugstore bag. Her fingers recognized with a pang the familiar outlines of the box she pulled out—a one-pound Sampler. The same thing they had bought for the landlady that afternoon.

"Oh!" The sudden pain of it stabbed her heart and eyes.

"It *is* beautiful, isn't it?" he said.

"I thought so," she answered, "when we bought one just like it for the landlady."

"And here we are . . . ," he was saying, rambling on, seeming not to have noticed the bitterness in her voice, nor the inappropriateness of his gift, "in our own room and our own bed, with our own Christmas tree, having our first Christmas together."

"Oh!" she cried again, the tears multiplying. "How could you! And *I* took such pains to please *you. I* shopped to buy the most for the money I had and you . . . *you* thought so little of me that you've given me the same old thing we gave the landlady. I never dreamed you were so cruel, so cruel and thoughtless!"

He seemed incapable of understanding even the plainest English. He was opening the box of chocolates, offering it to her reverently, as if the candies were pearls of great price and she a queen. "See how beautiful they are . . . ," he whispered, "like you."

But she cried on, inconsolable.

"On the inside of the lid, see—that's why they call it a *Sampler*—the chart identifies each piece. But if we don't read the chart—listen, sweetheart, if we only take each piece as it comes, why there's a whole box full of surprises here."

He took a chocolate from its fluted paper cup and held it out to her. It was wrapped in golden foil, and even in the dim light of the room it glistened. "Like our life together will be," he said. "We will take it as it comes, and there'll be many sweet surprises."

❉ ❉ ❉

One piece she kept for years in its Sampler box, wrapped in golden foil, its identity (like the years ahead) unknown. But the rest of the box they ate, one by one, with no chart to guide them, he kissing away her tears and telling her what their life would be. It was the happiest of all their Christmases.

He unwrapped this Sampler now, tearing away the

cellophane, while she remembered the sweet, sweet taste of chocolates and kisses that Christmas night, in a Murphy bed set on a floor of fir needles and gray moonlight.

Their children were plainly puzzled, since the significance of the candy was lost on them. How could they guess that there was nothing more in all the world to be given?

The torn cellophane fell to the floor, and she looked at him. He had leaned forward in his chair, as if waiting for something. The years had been many. She sat gazing at him, trying to guess his reaction to this silly, maudlin gift of hers. Just what had she expected? Then, suddenly, it seemed that all the rays of the weak December sun were drawn through the glass panes of the sun porch to converge upon her husband's glasses and upon the box of golden chocolates in his hands. Bursts of light in rippled waves of warmth assaulted her eyes painfully. Such a showy, pretentious bit of self-indulgent symbolism this gift had been. Whatever was she thinking of? And he was plainly puzzled, or hurt, or angry, or out of patience with her. This Christmas would be the worst, the *very worst*, of all their Christmases!

As she watched, blinking against the awful truth, he took a chocolate from its fluted cup. He turned it in his fingers for a moment and shafts of light shot from the golden foil. Then he handed the candy to her. It was sheathed in gold and blinding brightness, but as it passed from his hands to hers the brilliance of its light retreated, to glimmer deeply in secret happiness inside. It did not in any way assault her eyes, and a great peacefulness fell across her shoulders and slipped into her heart.

"There are many sweet surprises here," he said.

". . . Why, there are more than enough for the rest of our lives."

Dorothea Allen McKemie

Dorothea Allen McKemie wrote for popular magazines during the second half of the twentieth century.

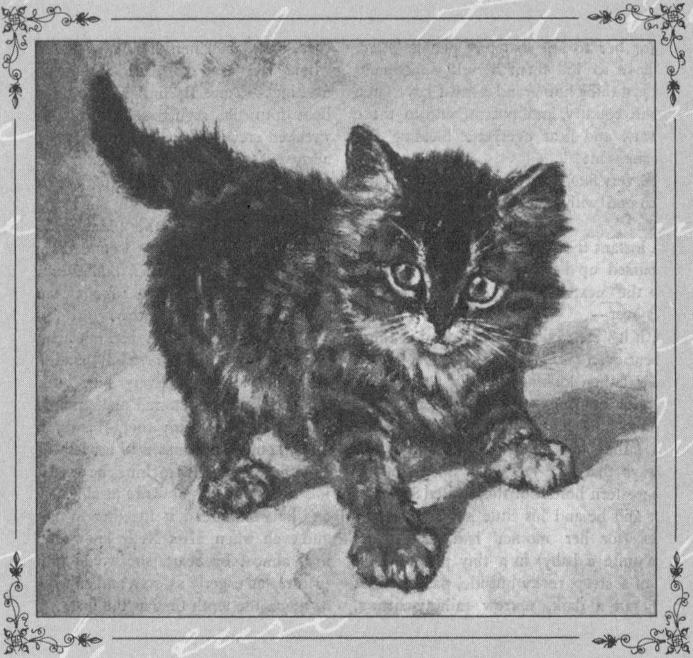

Ruth C. Ikerman

KITTEN OF BETHLEHEM

Kitten was tired, lonely, and hungry. If only just one person would take pity on him.

Then he heard the sound of an approaching donkey.

✳ ✳ ✳

One of the hardest types of Christmas story to find is one geared to very small children. This is just such a story.

When the innkeeper picked up a stone and tossed it at the furry tail, the kitten ran as fast as he could. He didn't stop until he reached the stable behind the inn.

Cautiously he poked his head around the corner to see if there was anyone inside who would make him move on. He was very tired and hungry. The only food he had found all day was a little milk in an indentation of a big rock where the goats had been milked. These belonged to a crowd of people who had just arrived.

There seemed to be lots of people coming into the town just now, with official-looking men bustling about to count them and their possessions. Kitten had played around the courtyard of the busy inn, hoping some of the strangers would stop to feed him, or at least notice him.

Now the innkeeper himself had shouted at him to get out of the way, and Kitten had barely managed to reach the stable. With his bright eyes, which could see well in the dark, he looked around to find out who was there ahead of him. Good! Here was a cow, and sometimes a little cat could make friends with a cow. If he stayed close when the good, rich milk was being taken, there might be some for him, too.

Over in the stable corner was the sturdy ox with his mate. A mother hen had gathered her chicks under her wings, and they were resting in the straw.

Silently surveying the leap it would be from the dusty ground to the warm manger straw, Kitten paused for strength, for he was weak from hunger. He took a big breath—then with a quick twist of his back feet he took off in a broad jump, and landed nimbly in the sweet-smelling hay. He treaded his bed with his front paws, then dropped his furry face in a moment of surrender and rest.

But soon he heard someone entering the stable. Could the innkeeper be hunting him? He jumped up and arched his back, making his tail twice its usual size. At least he would put up a good fight if the big dogs were turned loose on him.

Instead Kitten saw a tired little donkey entering the stable—the same kind of patient animal that had been bringing people into the inn courtyard. Kitten let his tail return to normal size before he scampered forward to welcome the newcomer. He knew what it was to be lonely and afraid, and he wanted to offer his friendship.

The donkey looked at him out of one big eye beneath a big ear, and the kitten looked back out of his eyes which could see in the dark. He said, "Welcome," in the sweetest tone of meow he could manage in his hunger.

The donkey halted as the man walking beside him said, "It's all right. Here we are now, with a roof over our heads, and shelter for the night."

The man was speaking to a woman seated on the donkey. Tenderly he lifted her down to the manger, and she gave a soft sigh of relief on reaching the straw. She closed her eyes and put her head back on the pillow of hay.

Kitten had never seen such a sweet, kind face. He crept closer. His paws moved a stray piece of straw that tickled the lady's arm. She opened her eyes and saw the kitten beside her. Gently the soft hands touched his head, and he felt the fear going out of him at the touch.

Holding fast to the kitten, she reached out to the man

beside the donkey and said, "Oh, see what we have found! A beautiful kitten waiting with us for our baby."

Suddenly the lonely kitten felt he was within the circle of a family. His heart pounded with the sheer joy of knowing that now he belonged to someone.

The man reached into the bag that hung from the side of the donkey and took out a little brown earthen bowl. Into it, he poured milk from a skin container. He crumbled a piece of brown bread into the liquid. Then he placed it on the ground and beckoned to the kitten.

How good the bread and milk tasted! Kitten tried not to take it all in greedy gulps. Methodically he cleaned the bowl, then withdrew on soft feet to the corner of the stable and soon was asleep.

When Kitten opened his eyes, he thought it must be morning, but the light which streamed into the open manger was not like any sunlight he had ever seen. Yet it was not like the night either, although there were stars overhead—the same stars under which he had traveled, weary and alone, hunting a home.

An unusual radiance streamed from the largest star of all, directly over the manger. And there lay a baby cradled beside the lady with the understanding eyes. Nearby stood the man, the weariness erased from his face in a moment of happy triumph over discouragement.

The cow chewed her cud rhythmically, and the breath of the oxen came in deep measures of satisfaction. A white chicken clucked and the others answered drowsily. Soon all were wide awake, for glorious music filled the stable.

It seemed to Kitten that the light was singing. Such

heavenly sounds he had never heard before. He felt he would burst if he couldn't join the hallelujahs of joy.

Kitten had never learned to sing, but he wanted to be part of this chorus. He took a deep breath and let the good air come into his tiny lungs. He began to purr in time with the song he heard. Louder swelled the chorus from on high. It was echoed in Kitten's sweet, harmonious purring.

The mother turned from looking at her child and saw again the kitten, his little ribs pressing out as he purred his lullaby for the new baby. She smiled at Kitten, and over him passed such a peace as he had never expected to find on this earth.

Thinking of the gifts he would find for the new baby, he looked up to see a white lamb approaching ahead of a shepherd with a crook. Kitten had seen such men in the hills, and sometimes one would share his food with a wandering kitten. Now a band of shepherds approached the manger as though guided by the star. They knelt and offered the beautiful lamb as a love gift.

Watching the shepherds presenting their gift to the baby, Kitten turned away in discouragement. What gift could he bring to the baby? He remembered the gentle touch of the beautiful lady, and the kindness of the man in sharing their food. There must be something he could give in return.

Deep in his heart he said, *I do not have anything to give except myself. I will give that gladly.* He moved to the foot of the manger and climbed the rough wood to the straw. He stretched out the full length of his furry coat to let its warmth comfort the tired feet of the lady, resting with the child in her arms. She put her head back and smiled. Kitten felt his heart warmed within him. His gift had been accepted in love, even as it had been offered.

He began to purr again in gratitude. He had found the rich satisfaction and peace that come from giving of oneself. Happily he closed his eyes to sleep, and to gather strength for the living of his new life, which would be forever marked by the echo of the wonderful song.

Ruth C. Ikerman

Ruth C. Ikerman, besides her editorial work, wrote prolifically for popular and inspirational magazines during the second half of the twentieth century.

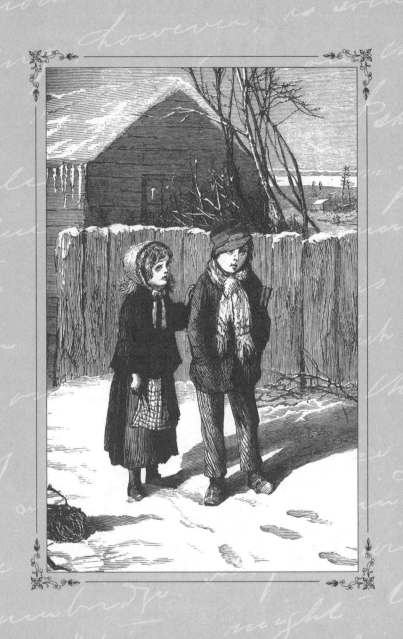

Author Unknown

EMPTY BOXES

---

*What a wagonload of Christmas presents Father
would bring home with him. After all, he had two
twenty-dollar gold pieces in his pocket (a small fortune
in those days).*

*But neither Father nor his team of horses returned
home until Christmas morning. And in the wagon
were only empty boxes.*

*Yet . . . it was "the best Christmas she would ever
have."*

*C*hristmas had always been different for Christina and Albert Ross.

They had no aunts, no uncles, and no cousins to come and bring them gifts. All they had was their mother.

Yet Albert and Christina did have a grandmother.

She lived on a ranch out in Oregon, thousands of miles away. They never expected to see her; however, they knew she loved and cared for them. Every Christmas, she sent big boxes filled with cookies and exactly the kinds of toys they wanted.

The Christmas Albert was almost nine and Christina five and a half their grandmother wrote: "This year I am not sending packages, I am coming to see you."

"She might bring the presents with her," Christina said hopefully to Albert.

Albert, who got A's in math and could count money, said, "Don't plan on it, kid. It costs so much to come so far, she probably won't be able to buy presents."

Christina, who wanted a doll, began to cry. "Hush," said her mother. "You children should learn presents are not what Christmas is all about."

"Yeah, we know," said Albert, who liked to talk back to his mother. "Everybody says that." Albert wanted an airplane with a real motor, an airplane that could really fly.

Christmas morning, Albert and Christina had to wait to open their presents until Grandmother came. They were allowed to shake their packages, but there wasn't one that felt like a doll or an airplane with a motor. They were all soft packages, like clothes!

They left for the railroad station right after breakfast. Albert spotted a tiny, smiling woman with twinkly blue eyes and wavy grey hair. "That's her, that's her," he cried. When their mother rushed forward to greet Grandmother, Albert, who remembered his father, whispered to Christina, "Her eyes are just like Dad's. I would have known her anywhere." Christina, who had been born after her father died, eagerly searched her grandmother's face.

Christina noticed Grandmother carried only a little handbag, far too small to contain a big doll. Albert was right. Grandmother had spent all her Christmas money to come see them. But then Grandmother opened her handbag and took out small pieces of cardboard with numbers on them. These she exchanged at a window marked "baggage" for a suitcase and a wooden box with metal corners and leather straps.

"This is my mother's old quilt chest," she said. "I thought you might want it." Christina looked at the chest. Albert looked at the chest. It was big enough to hold a very large doll and an airplane too.

The taxi driver could hardly get the chest in the trunk. It stuck out the back.

Home, at the apartment, Grandmother asked Albert to open the chest. In it was box after box with everything he and Christina had wanted for Christmas. There were even some things they had not thought of wanting. All the boxes were wrapped with pretty paper and tied with ribbons.

After all the packages were opened, the floor of the little living room was covered with boxes and papers. "Children," said their mother, "while I set the table, you pick up all the papers and boxes and take them out to the garbage."

"No!" Grandmother looked shocked. "No! No! No! The paper is too pretty to throw away. Tomorrow I will iron it out. You can always use the boxes."

Christina heard her mother say, "Nobody saves used Christmas paper anymore. And we have so little room."

Grandmother answered firmly, "But *I* save it. I always have and I always will! It isn't just the money the paper and the boxes cost. It is something else . . . like the memory of the best Christmas I ever had."

Albert handed his grandmother the holly paper that had held his skateboard box. She smoothed it carefully over her knee. "When I was a child, paper was precious. This is like the wallpaper I had on my first dollhouse. I was just Christina's age then. Five."

Grandmother's hands were shaking ever so slightly. There were tears in the corners of her eyes. Albert said quickly, "Tell us about the best Christmas you ever had. What did you get?"

"Nothing," she said. "Nothing." Tears rolled down her cheeks.

"No presents at all?" Albert could hardly believe it.

"Not any." Grandmother wiped her eyes. "We were to have had many of them. But as it turned out we didn't. Yet it was the happiest Christmas I ever had. Later, when I grew older and heard the story of The Other Wise Man, I knew my father was like him."

"I know about The Other Wise Man," Albert said eagerly. "He stopped so many times to do good for people, he never got where he was going on time."

"That is exactly what happened to my father. He started out to buy presents for us, but . . ."

"Tell us! Tell us, Grandma!" Christina jumped up and down. "Tell us!"

The children's mother had been listening as she set the table. She said, "What does that have to do with saving used Christmas paper and used Christmas boxes?"

"Everything," Grandmother chuckled. "Everything. We lived back in the Blue Mountains. It was a long way even to Henryville, the nearest settlement. There is nothing there now. But then, there was a general store, a post office, and a railroad. The train stopped once a day, late in the afternoon. A stagecoach went through Henryville, too. It was one of the last of the old horse-drawn rock-a-byes that operated in the United States. The roads in the Blue Mountains then were rocky and steep, and in the winter, especially, autos couldn't get through.

"The year I was five, going on six, it began to snow early in December. A few days before Christmas, we could only see the top rail on the fences. We were snow-bound. Then it turned cold and a crust formed on the snow that was so hard it could hold up a team. Father said he would take the big bobsled and go to Henryville to get our Christmas things.

"Mr. Henry, the man the town was named after, owned the general store. He always laid in lots of things for Christmas—dolls from Germany for the little girls, BB guns for the smaller boys and .22 rifles for the bigger ones, ice skates, sleds, little rocking chairs, and story books with colored pictures. There were peppermint sticks, lemon sticks, and wooden buckets of rock candy with roses in the center.

"When Father started early the morning before Christmas for Henryville, he had two shiny $20 gold pieces in his pocket. Back in November, our Grandmother Curtis had sent them—one for me and one for my brother, Joel. She said she wanted us to have a wonderful Christmas, but also to learn to share and show the love of Christ.

"In those days, $20 was a fortune. Joel and I talked about what we would give others, and what we would get for ourselves. We finally decided we would each give $2 to the circuit rider and get presents for Mother and Father. The rest we would have for ourselves. Father claimed he wanted a pair of mittens and a cap. Mother said she was tired of venison and wanted a turkey, two pounds of cranberries, and five pounds of powdered sugar. Joel wanted a .22 rifle. I had my heart set on a blue-eyed doll, a cart for her, and some candy hearts with writing on them.

"The last thing I heard Father say to Mother as he left was, 'It should be a good Christmas with all this money to spend. I just *have* to get to Henryville.'

"'Don't forget the turkey,' Mother cautioned. Father grinned and snapped the lines. 'It will be late before I get back, but don't worry.'

"All that day, we dreamed about Christmas, the turkey dinner, the toys. We strung popcorn for our Christmas tree and made paper dolls out of old newspapers. We tied on red apples, and Mother let us have one sheet of her white writing paper to make an angel for the top.

"She let us stay up past our eight o'clock bedtime, but at ten, Father still had not come, so we had to go to bed. 'God will take care of Father,' Mother said. 'He will be here in the morning.'

"It was just barely light when Joel woke me up. 'Get up, sleepyhead, it's Christmas!' Then he ran downstairs in his nightshirt. I followed close behind. There was our Christmas tree with its paper dolls and popcorn strings, but no presents under it. 'Father hasn't come yet,' Mother said. 'I can't imagine what is keeping him, but go upstairs and dress. He will be along by and by.' Mother made her special six-egg hotcakes for our breakfast and spread them with huckleberry syrup. 'Father will be here soon,' she kept saying.

"We were almost through eating when we heard the sleigh bells. We ran to the window and in a few minutes saw the team coming around the hill and through the trees. The crusty snow was sparkling and the old bobsled was loaded with every kind of box you could imagine. They were piled higher than Father's head, and some were stacked on the seat beside him.

"'Thank you, God,' I heard Mother say right out loud. 'Thank you for bringing him home safe.' Father pulled up by the door and jumped out of the sled.

"'Whatever kept you so long?' Mother asked, and gave him a big kiss before he had time to answer.

"'Merry Christmas,' my brother and I shouted. 'Merry Christmas.'

"'I'll unhitch here,' Father said, 'so it will be easier to unload. Joel, you take the horses to the barn. Alice, help him and measure out the grain.'

"I ran to the house for mittens and stocking cap. When I came out, Joel was already at the barn with Babe and Sis. Neither Father nor Mother seemed to notice me. I heard Mother say, 'What did you buy with $40 to fill so many boxes?'

"Then Father said, 'I didn't buy anything. Nothing. When I got to the store, it was closed and locked. The boxes are all empty.'

"In all my life since, I have never been so stunned. We weren't going to get anything for Christmas!

"Joel was struggling to lift the heavy harness up on the pegs as I trudged into the barn. 'We aren't going to get any Christmas presents.' I said. 'All the boxes are empty. I heard Father tell Mother so.'

"Joel laughed. 'Cheer up, kid,' he said. 'That was just fooling. You know how folks joke about Santa Claus.'

"'No, it is real. The boxes are empty. They were talking. They didn't know I heard.'

"'You're crazy.' That was all Joel could think of to say. 'You're crazy!'

"We hurried back to the house. Father was sitting at the kitchen table, drinking a cup of hot milk. Mother was stirring up what was left of the six-egg hotcake batter and warming the syrup. Mother said, 'You'll have to explain to the children. I hope you can make them understand.'

"Then she turned to us. 'Your Father is very tired. He has had a hard time. He has come home without any presents, without the $20 gold pieces, or my turkey. But I am sure he did the right thing. Now he wants to tell you what happened.'

"Father took a big gulp of milk and wiped his mouth with a napkin. Then I heard Joel's voice waver. 'I wanted a .22. Where is my .22?'

"'Calm down, Son,' Father said sternly, 'so I can tell you.'

"'I wanted a blue-eyed doll!' I screamed. 'A blue-eyed doll.'

"'Be quiet,' Mother warned, 'or I'll send you both upstairs to bed, even if it is Christmas. Things don't always go as planned.'

"Mother wiped my eyes on her apron and took me up on her lap. Joel settled sullenly into a straight chair. All the joys of Christmas seemed to have departed.

"'As you know, I left early,' Father began. 'I had been on the road about an hour when I came to Dr. Turner's cutter. He was trying to get up Copper Canyon to deliver Mrs. Steven's baby. One of the tugs was broken and he had no way to fix it. I spent two hours helping him get going. So that gave me a slow start, but I figured I still had plenty of time to get to Henryville. Dr. Turner asked me to be on the lookout for a new family that had just moved into the Wilson Mine. He had told them they must get their twin sons to a hospital in Portland. He thought I might pass them on the way.

"'When I came to the main road in the alley,' Father continued, 'the snow wasn't nearly so deep and the road had been packed down by travel. There was a stagecoach with a wheel off. The driver was just a young fellow and wasn't sure of himself, so I fixed the wheel and lost some more time.

"'He gave me $2 for my trouble. I didn't want to take it, but he said it was a Christmas present for my children. I figured I would get a bucket of hard candy with it. The stage went on ahead of me while I picked up my tools.

"'It wasn't long before I overtook the folks from the Wilson Mine. They had a balky old horse and wagon and were having trouble. The horse wouldn't go. The man hailed me down and asked if I would take him and his wife and three children to the train. I saw only one child, a girl about two years old, so I asked where the other two were. The woman was crying. She led me to the back of the wagon, and there were two little twin boys in a box covered with a quilt. Both boys were wrapped up so tight all I could see was their heads. I reckon they were about Alice's age, fair-haired little tykes and terribly sick. It looked to me like they wouldn't make it unless something was done. They both had high fevers, but it seemed like one was much worse than the other.

"'It was about the saddest thing I have ever seen. The mother was worn out, having been up night and day. The father was sick with worry, straining to catch the train. The boys were dying and the old horse wouldn't go.

"'I told them to pull off the road, unhitch, and let the horse go back home. Then we put the box with the boys in it in the bobsled. The mother and father got in. The little girl was crying with the cold. I whopped Old Babe and Sis. It seemed like they knew we needed to make good time. I have never known them to go faster, and we made it to the train almost half an hour early.

"'The conductor didn't want to take the boys on account of what they had might be catching. But he gave in when he read the letter the folks had from Dr. Turner. He said there wouldn't be anyone in the caboose, and they could all ride in there. Then it turned out they didn't have enough money for fares for all of them. The father could go, or the mother, but not both.

The sick boys needed their mother, but I didn't see how she could manage without their father. So I gave them the two $20 gold pieces and the $2 I got for fixing the stagecoach wheel!'

"Then Joel interrupted Father. 'But wasn't that more than they needed? They already had enough to pay one fare. You said so.'

"'Yes, Son,' Father nodded. 'But I knew they would need some place to stay and something to eat. I knew they would need money for medicine and for the hospital!'

"'So you gave them the grocery money, too,' Mother said.

"Father looked miserable. 'You would have done the same thing,' he said, 'if you had seen those two little boys. One of them looked at me like that last deer I shot. I couldn't stand it.' He paused. I saw Mother squeeze his hand. 'Old man Henry is always asking me if I want credit. I have always said I didn't, but I figured this time I would take him up on it so we could have a Christmas and help the folks, too.'

"'What about the little girl?' Mother asked.

"'They wanted me to take her to the postmistress. So I did. I figured I could still get to the store before closing. But when I got there, the store was locked up. I knocked on the window, figuring somebody would come and open up, but there was nobody there. Job Betts came along and told me Mr. Henry had about sold all the holiday things out, so he had closed up early and gone on the stage to Mayville to be with his children for Christmas.'

"'That was the stage you fixed the wheel for,' Joel

said. 'If you hadn't done that, we would at least have had some Christmas. Now I won't ever get my .22.'

"I could tell Joel was terribly upset about his gun. 'It wasn't your money to give away,' he blurted out. 'One of those $20 gold pieces was mine!'

"'Yes, Son,' Father said. 'I thought of that. But you know, those two $20 gold pieces were wrapped up in your grandmother's letter. I got it out and read it over before I gave them away. The letter said the money was to be used for your Christmas, and to teach you the real meaning of giving, and the joy of Christ. I figured saving the lives of two helpless children might do just that.'

"I could see Joel was moved, but he was still thinking about the rifle he wouldn't have. 'I guess I can get a gun anytime,' he muttered. Mother put her hand on his shoulder. He turned his head quickly. Joel didn't want me to see his tears.

"'When I took the little girl to the postmistress,' Father said, 'she told me she didn't have a thing for a child for Christmas. I told her I'd get a little something at the store, but I didn't know then the store was closed. I had to go back and tell her I couldn't get anything. She said it didn't seem like Mr. Henry to close early on Christmas Eve. So I went back and rattled the lock again. After that I went around back and rapped, but nobody answered.

"'Then I saw all the packing boxes they had thrown out. I guess I was just desperate. I didn't want to come home without something, so I loaded them up. It seemed like I just had to have something to fetch. When I was putting them on the sled, a broken doll fell out of one of them. Both its arms were off and one leg was damaged, but I thought it could be fixed. The head was good.'

"'My baby doll!' I shrieked. 'My blue-eyed doll. Where is it?'

"Father took me on his knee. 'Honey child,' he said, 'I took it to the little girl. The postmistress said she could fix it. I told her my Alice wanted a blue-eyed doll like it, but she was a big girl now, five years old, almost six. And she would be with her mother and father at Christmas, so she would like little Mary to have it.'

"'Her name is Mary?'

"Father nodded. 'Yes, Mary, like the Christmas baby's mother!'

"'It is better to give than to get,' Mother said, and I felt her hand on my head. 'My little girl must learn that. It is what Christmas is about. The Christmas baby gave His life for us.'

"Suddenly Father sat me on the floor. 'I have an idea. Let's unload the sled. Four of those boxes nailed together would make a wonderful doll house.'

"'I can find stuff in the rag bag for rugs and curtains,' Mother said. 'We could make furniture out of shoe boxes.'

"'There is an oak box out there,' Father announced, 'that looked to me like with some beeswax and a little fixing would make a good Flyer.'

"Joel ran out and started taking things off the bobsled. The boxes were not all entirely empty. Some had crumpled-up wrapping paper in them, and there were even a few pieces of rumpled tissue and bits of excelsior that Mother said would be good for doll bed mattresses. One box had three magazines with the covers torn off, and another had some pieces of Christmas wrapping paper with holly berries on it. We carried the boxes into the house.

"Father had nested some of them, so there were boxes inside of boxes. Shoe boxes. Hat boxes. Soap boxes. Cardboard boxes. But mostly they were wooden boxes. Cigar boxes, round cheese boxes with lids. There were even candy buckets with tiny, tiny pieces of hard candy sticking to them inside. There were a couple of nail kegs, a good barrel, and a broken barrel. There was about every kind of container you could think of. Joel claimed one for a tool box and Mother found one for a quilt chest. I stacked up four for a doll house.

"Father hid in one of the biggest wooden packing boxes, and when Mother lifted the lid, he jumped up like a jack-in-the-box. Suddenly we were all laughing and planning what we would do with our boxes.

"Mother seemed to have forgotten about her turkey and cranberries. 'How would you like potato pancakes for dinner?'

"'Great,' Father answered, 'with dried peaches and cheese dumplings afterwards.'

"We spent all day Christmas playing with the boxes. One box had a piece of pink tissue paper left in it, and Mother showed us how to make a peep show. We made a little hole in one end of a shoe box. On the inside at the other end, we pasted pictures of mountains cut from the old magazines. Then we mounted pictures of people and animals on light cardboard and set them up inside. Then the pink tissue paper was pasted over the top of the box, and when we peeked in, there was an enchanted world we had created ourselves.

"Father showed me how to play I was a rocking horse by putting one foot on each end of a stave from the broken barrel. Joel got inside the good barrel and rolled down the hill a dozen times. Mother helped me make tables and chairs for my doll house, and she got out her needles and embroidery thread and began to make the head of a blue-eyed doll. It had pigtails of yellow yarn.

"It was fun playing with Mother and Father and the boxes . . . the most fun we ever had. But every once in a while I could see Mother was near tears. She could not forget those little sick boys in the box on the train. She kept saying to Father, 'I'm glad you did what you did.'

"And that," finished Grandmother, folding a piece of gold foil Christmas wrap, "was the best Christmas we ever had. Some other Christmases I can't even remember. The next year, Joel got his .22, and I got my blue-eyed doll. It had real hair and would go to sleep when I laid it down, but somehow I never loved it quite as much as the one Mother made for me."

"Tell us," said Christina, "what happened to the two little boys in the box. Did they live?"

Grandmother's eyes lowered. "One of them died on the train before they got to Portland. But the doctors managed to save the other one."

"What happened to him?" Albert asked, as he stroked the wings of his new airplane.

Grandmother smiled. "Lots of things. When I grew up, I married him. He was your grandfather. If it hadn't been for that empty box Christmas, you wouldn't be here."

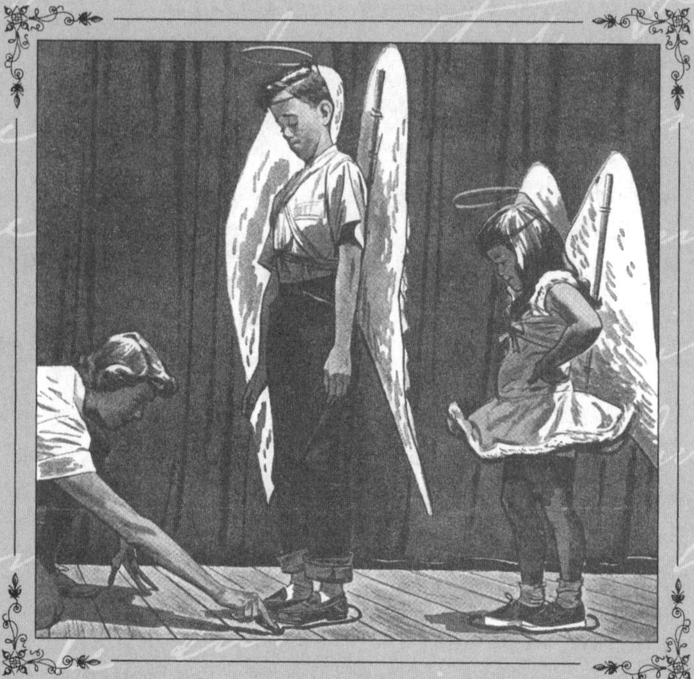

Mary Geisler Phillips

SURPRISE CHRISTMAS

---

*The town was split right down the middle—and
hardly anyone spoke with anyone across the line.
Then two strangers came into town. So car-trouble
met with heart-trouble.*

❄ ❄ ❄

*Just recently my Great Aunt Lois Wheeler Berry sent
me this old story. My late grandmother, Ruby Wheeler,
had copied it out by hand. And this story is the only
thing I own in her handwriting. Needless to say, it
is precious.*

*C*hristmas does something to people if they let it. At least it made a big difference to all of the two hundred families in our town of Opunta last year.

This is what happened out here in the desert, where the highway runs straight as a string across New Mexico. Christmas for us usually isn't very different from other days, for nobody has much money to spend, and trees are scarce.

Well, Christmas came on Monday, and the Saturday morning before, Em Tibbetts and I were sitting on the old cot in the garage that our husbands own together. They call it "Desert Garage," and it's the only one for miles along the highway.

I always like to look at Em. Her blue eyes are gentle and kind, and her black hair goes smoothly back from a center part. She had on her old brown coat, although we had a fire going in the oil drum we use for a stove. She could no longer button the coat around her swollen body, for her baby was almost due.

"Would you like a Christmas baby, Em—a boy?" I asked. Her two little girls were playing at the back of the garage, where Gus had made them a large work table.

"Yes," she said softly, and her face lighted up, then turned sad. "But I'm glad the hospital is not in this dreadful town. I couldn't bear to have him born here where there is so much hatefulness."

Em and Curly live on a ranch five miles out of Opunta, and she had been patiently sitting all day in the garage for the past week, so that if she were taken, Curly could rush her to the hospital forty miles away. I envied her, with her two children and another coming. Our only son went down with his plane in the Pacific Ocean.

Oh, I couldn't bear the thought of Christmas coming without Johnny—he loved it so! I disliked the town too. I looked at the highway that divided the two parts of Opunta, and at the Cochise Mountains gaunt against the blue sky. They were grim and bitter, like me. On the other side of the road lived Elsie Gallegher, who used to be my best friend, but I hadn't spoken to her for three years. The town fight had finally separated even us.

Curly was whistling as he worked in the pit, when my Gus appeared at the doorway. We live in a trailer right next to the garage.

"Hi!" he greeted us. He stays cheerful, no matter how disgruntled I get. Just then a car with a New York license limped into the space in front of the garage.

"Sounds like a broken piston," Gus said, and Curly added: "At least one!"

A middle-aged couple stepped out of the car. The man was wearing one of those dark red sport shirts and gray pants. The woman was short and plump, and looked as if she laughed a lot. Her gray hair was short and fluffy, and her skin was like a child's.

"Good morning!" the tall man said. "We're in trouble—can you help us?"

"Morning," Curly replied. "We can try, but that engine sounds pretty well chewed up."

❄ ❄ ❄

Well, it turned out they'd have to have a new engine. Curly 'phoned, and located a place that had one, in the town where the hospital is.

Dr. and Mrs. Bell, the owners of the car, took the

news that they wouldn't reach their family in Phoenix for Christmas Day like good sports, but I could see how disappointed they were. Mrs. Bell went to the doorway and looked across the highway.

"Are those tourist cabins over there?"

"Yes," I said. "The only ones in town. That grey house next to the filling station is where the Galleghers live—they're the owners."

As she tripped across the road the red handkerchief around her neck reminded me of the cardinal that comes around my step for crumbs.

❄ ❄ ❄

I went back home to start my dinner, and when I opened the door of the trailer, I faced the picture of Johnny's smiling face. I had to do something with my hands quick. So I went to the kitchen and started making the Christmas cookies.

The night before, Gus had said: "Have you asked Curly's family for Christmas dinner?"

"No—nothing doing," I replied.

"Look, it'll be good to have the children around."

I went on knitting, listening to cars whizzing by, taking folks home for Christmas. But then, at bedtime, I looked out the window. The moon was up, nearly full, and the mountain peaks had a pale, peaceful, faraway look. I turned to Gus, ashamed.

"Okay, Gus, if you want the Tibbetts, we'll have them for dinner."

"Atta girl! Swell!" he said, getting into bed and pulling up the pieced quilt.

I kept thinking of the old Christmases. I longed for trees with snow on the branches, crunching feet in the snow, the smell of Johnny's wool mittens drying after coasting.

Thinking of those days, I tried to pray, facing the thin moonlight.

❄ ❄ ❄

It was the next day the Bells had arrived, Saturday. I overslept that night, and when I got up on Sunday, Gus was already at the garage.

I opened the trailer door to the sunshine, and there was Mrs. Bell heading my way.

"Good morning, Mrs. Todd! The men tell me our car won't be ready until Tuesday."

Then after a pause: "Is there a grocery store open on Sunday?"

"Yes," I said, "on that cross street, up half a block."

She started off, then called back: "Do you have a service any time today in that little church down the street?"

I shook my head. "No service today."

"Oh, I'm sorry. It won't seem like Christmas without a tree and without carols. Without a turkey and a big family around the table, too!"

I said: "We only get a visiting preacher now and then."

"For goodness sake! You mean the church won't even be *lighted?*"

❄ ❄ ❄

Later, on my way to the garage to help the men, I saw her going up her path with a big paper bag in her arms.

She called across, as if we'd known each other all our lives.

"I got the last quart of milk, and the last can of orange juice. Got bologna, cheese and crackers, too!"

I thought of my roasting chicken and mince pie. I called "Good!" for politeness, and went on wondering how long the engine job would take. The old engine was on the block and tackle ready to lift out.

Em was there watching, and Dr. Bell sat on the cot with her, joshing back and forth with our men. I went over to the stove and dripped a little more oil in the drum. The fire felt good—the thermometer must have been down in the fifties.

Just then, Mrs. Bell came in. "Good morning!" she said. "Curly, who has the key to the church?"

"I do, ma'am—I keep the place clean."

"If you'll open it," she said, "and I can find a boy to drive to the mountains and get a tree, tonight we'll have something in that church that looks like Christmas."

Curly and Gus looked at each other.

Mrs. Bell went on: "We'll get in the neighbors . . ."

"Wait!" Em smoothed her glossy hair with a hand that trembled. "*You* tell her," and she nodded at me.

I gave it to her straight.

"Our town's split in two—the Irish, who live mostly on the other side of the highway, fight with us on this side— we're of English descent. They're the Gallegher Gang— they call us the Tibbetts Toughs. The fight began years ago over the location of the new school house."

Em added sadly: "Now the two groups won't agree about anything."

Mrs. Bell just stood there and stared at us. There wasn't a sound. Suddenly her face changed as if the sun had come out.

"But it's *Christmas!* Maybe—anyway, I'm going ahead! Is that young fellow across the road one of the Gallegher Gang?" I nodded. "Then he's my man to go for the tree!" And she was out of the door like a shot. Soon she was back with two boys who were tickled to go, using Gus's car.

Next she wrote an invitation for everyone to come to the carol sing, and sent Em's little girls around the town with it, stopping at every house. As Leona and Carol set off, Mrs. Bell said: "Tell all the children you see that we need their help right away to make paper chains. We'll meet in the Sunday-school room."

Her husband said, "I'll go to the store and get colored wrappings, paste, and scissors."

And Gus said: "Get some tin cans, too. I've got tin shears to cut out tin stars."

Mrs. Bell's cheeks were pink. "You'll help, won't you?" she said to Em and me.

"Sorry, but I've got to help here," I said, not looking at her. But Curly had to pipe up, "Go ahead, Martha. I'm goin' over to open the church and clean up."

So there was nothing I could do but go along.

When the boys came back with the tree Mrs. Bell said: "Thank you, boys! See you tonight!"

Harry scratched his arm. John shuffled his feet, hesitated, and then spoke: "No'em, don't believe so. Our folks won't let us. G'bye!"

Mrs. Bell looked tired. But when Carol and Leona came in she brightened.

"How would you little girls like to be dressed up like angels tonight?" she asked. They both jumped up, yelling "Yes! Yes!"

It was a busy afternoon, and there was no time to make real costumes. The wings and one robe were all we could manage.

Later, when Em and I got back to the garage, Mrs. Bell joined us.

"Well, I've had fun making friends all over town!" she said. "I have three Gallegher kings, one Gallegher shepherd, and Joseph! A lot of Gallegher angels, too."

We all laughed, she looked so pleased with herself.

"Oh yes, and Mary is to be Judy Gallegher, that pretty blonde."

"Not *Judy!* Of all things!" I cried.

"Uh-huh. I've unwrapped the big doll we have for our grandchild for the manger, and the new family in town—the Darlingtons—are lending me gold-colored draperies for the kings' robes." Her face glowed.

I knew everyone would be dying to go, for we hadn't had anything like this in Opunta for years. Maybe they'd let the kids take part, but no Gallegher family grown-up would attend. I kept wondering what I could do. And then it came to me. I guess I had been as stubborn as anybody else in the town fight.

I got out the three pot-holders I had made for friends who'd never get them now. I took off my apron, put

them in my bag and crossed to Galleghers' door. Elsie
opened the door and looked at me as if she had never
seen me before. I held out the red package.

"Here, Elsie. Merry Christmas!"

She stammered: "Why—why—thank you, Martha!
Come on in!"

I stepped inside, and a warm feeling came over me. I
looked away and noticed the rug.

"You've got a new rug!" I got out finally, and then we
laughed and started to talk, both at once, like old times.

I hurried on, "Did you know Mrs. Bell has got a lot
of families from your side of town to let their children
take part and to get together with us tonight?"

I hoped God would forgive me the white lie, for as
soon as I left Elsie, I went to Barnums' and Drakes' and
repeated it. I gave each wife a pot holder.

❋ ❋ ❋

As soon as dinner was over, we went to the church.
Young Mrs. Darlington turned up soon, friendly as you
please. Children rushed around, shrill and excited. Mrs.
Bell and Mrs. Darlington marked with chalk where they
were to stand.

Neighbors who had not spoken to each other for
years sat side by side, not looking at each other at first.
But when Mrs. Bell began playing "Silent Night," and
Gus and Dr. Bell pulled back the curtains, there was a
sigh, and everybody let go and smiled. Judy had her
hands clasped across her breast, her eyes adoring that
doll. Gus's spotlight made the children look almost like
real angels.

Then a little murmur of *Ohs* and *Ahs* ran through the pews.

So it had to be shown again, and after the curtains were pulled for the last time, everyone talked to everyone else. Such a hubbub!

❄ ❄ ❄

A little later, Mr. Darlington led us in the singing of the old favorites—children and grown-ups from both sides of town, singing *together*.

Just then Curly came in the side door, lifted the manger off the platform, and hurried out again. His face was tense and he didn't see anyone.

I looked around. Dr. and Mrs. Bell had disappeared too. Em had gone back some time before, taking the sleepy little girls. I slipped out and hurried toward the garage. I met Carol and Leona coming toward me.

"We've got a baby brother!"

"He's in the manger just like the baby Jesus!"

In the garage Dr. and Mrs. Bell were at the sink with towels around their heads and sleeves rolled up. On the cot, under blankets from the cabin, lay Em, looking up at Curly. In the manger was a small bundle.

I shut the door tight, for I could hear steps. The news had spread, and everyone was hurrying toward the garage. They stood at the door. Curly opened it a little, and someone whispered: "Has Em's child come?"

Curly nodded. "She'd like you to sing," he said.

Mr. Darlington began "Hark! The Herald Angels Sing!" We all joined in. I turned to the mountains with the light of the full moon on them. They had never looked so beautiful.

I thought: *They've seen many a birth! And many a mother weeping for her lost son. I am not alone—everyone knows sorrow at some time—it's how you take it that counts.*

Mary Geisler Phillips

Mary Geisler Phillips wrote for popular magazines during the middle of the twentieth century.

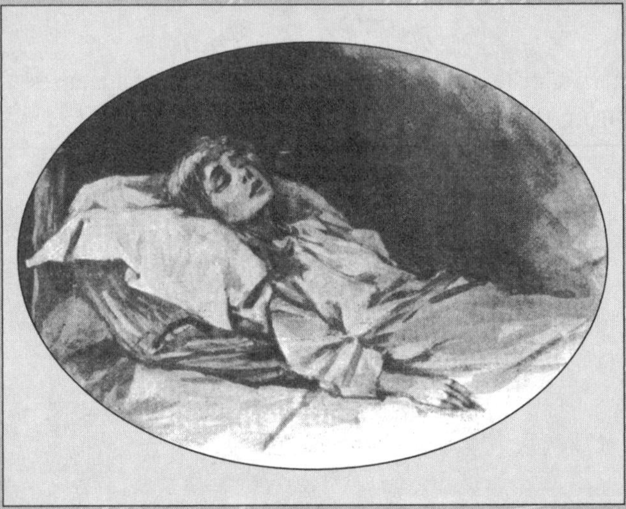

Christine Helsby as told to Ed Erny

OUR POW CHRISTMAS

The Japanese had conquered much of China, and Chiang Kai-shek withdrew his armies to Chungking. A young missionary couple were held as prisoners of war in a Japanese prison camp. They almost despaired, that Christmas of 1944. Being destitute, how in the world could they give gifts to each other?

*W*hen I came to consciousness that chilly Christmas morning, I could almost feel the grey light seeping through the window just above my head. I turned to look out at the great stretches of brick wall, bristling with strands of electrified barbed wire and broken at intervals by menacing pillboxes, manned by one of the omnipresent olive-uniformed Japanese guards. Within the wall of this former mission compound now lived a community of ill-fed, ill-clothed prisoners.

This was December 25, 1944, and I was lying on a rough grass mattress in the camp hospital, where I had been taken two weeks earlier for internal bleeding. An adjoining building served as a barracks for the mentally ill, and to one side of it lay a melancholy plot of ground which enfolded the swelling population of our dead.

My husband, Meredith, and I had come as missionaries to Peking in October 1940. Less than two months later our first child, Sandra Kay, was born. We had completed only one term of language study before Pearl Harbor. Suddenly we found ourselves prisoners of war. Following 14 months of house arrest we were shipped by rail to Wei Hsien, a small village on the east coast near the port of Ching Dao. There on the compound, newly converted into a prisoner of war camp, we were joined by 1,800 fellow internees—500 of them missionaries, the remainder of them business people.

The long wall which ran its irregular course around the camp marked, for us, the outer limits of our world. Now, for 33 long months, we had been cut off from all reliable news sources. Were the Allies winning the war? Losing the war? How much longer would we have to endure this ordeal? Not one of us knew. Few dared guess. Hope was hard to come by that bleak December. But this morning would be different, must be different. This was Christmas Day.

Now the pale morning light, like a persistent hand, was stirring patients from their fitful sleep. Beside me I could hear the moans of an older woman suffering from pleurisy. Beyond her another patient, a pneumonia case, struggled for breath. Directly across from me a young mother was apparently dying of typhoid fever.

There were 16 beds and 16 patients in that barn-like women's ward. The once well-furnished hospital had been left a shambles by troops who had been quartered there some months earlier. Now the building was crudely sectioned off into two large wards. Heroic doctors and nurses, themselves prisoners, gave unstintingly of their skill; but with almost no medicine available, too often their best efforts ended in futility. For the most part, the old hospital served only to quarantine the sick and dying from the still-functioning members of our community.

Meredith worked as a cook in the main kitchen, one of the many tasks performed by prisoners who operated all the basic services of the camp. He was permitted to take one hour off between breakfast and lunch. We had agreed that during that time he would bring Sandy and the gifts to my bedside.

My gift for Meredith that Christmas was to be a well-thumbed but still-sturdy copy of *Matthew's Chinese-English Dictionary*, a book he long had coveted but never felt he could afford. I had discovered it at The White Elephant, a brick cubicle where outgrown and expendable commodities could be sold or bartered. The price was a full $10. For us, that was a lot of money at any time, but in camp, where a rare "monthly" Red Cross allowance of $5 was our only source of income, it was a fortune. I knew, however, that when the cash price for an item could not be met, the seller would often settle for the balance in accepted barter.

What could I barter? I went to our little black foot-locker, one of the two pieces of luggage we had been permitted to bring into camp. There, in a corner, was all that remained of our little store of goods. Quickly I took inventory, then took out a yard of new cloth and my prize can of strawberry jam. I had $2 in my pocket and felt sure a friend would loan me two more. With these, I bought *Matthew's Dictionary*.

Now I heard Meredith's familiar footsteps approaching from the far end of the ward and looked up. He was wearing a rough plaid mackinaw and too-short pants—both held together by patch on patch.

Sandy skipped beside him, her blonde curls bobbing, her brown eyes unnaturally large but glowing with excitement against her thin features. She wore dark blue overalls I had fashioned from upholstery material. Her coat had been made from the remains of a fellow missionary's tweed skirt. Together Meredith and Sandy clutched their presents, all wrapped in used notebook paper.

"Oh, Mommy," Sandy shouted gaily, "isn't it wonderful? It's Christmas. Look, we brought presents!"

Meredith and Sandy sat beside me. A nurse thoughtfully procured the hospital's only screen and set it up against the foot of my bed for privacy. Now we were a family again. We were in our own world, and it was Christmas morning.

Meredith opened his pocket New Testament to the

familiar account: "And it came to pass in those days that there went out a decree from Caesar Augustus, that all the world should be taxed. . . ." Then we prayed.

"Mommy, Mommy! Can we have our presents now?" Sandy's little fingers were pulling impatiently at the stiff wraps.

Her "big gift" that Christmas was a wheelbarrow which Meredith had made from an old soap box. The single wheel had been purloined from the baby bed. The handles were scraps of wood gleaned from who-knows-where. Cliff, a camp teenager, had decorated the front of the barrow with a sketch of a bushy-tailed squirrel and Sandy's name in great block letters.

By any standard, it was a crude contraption. But to a four-year-old who had never seen a dime store, an ice-cream cone, or a dolly that opens its eyes and wets, it was a treasure.

Sandy got other gifts, too. From a scrap of cloth, no longer serviceable for mending garments, I had made a humpty-dumpty doll and had stuffed it with bits of thread and material swept from the community sewing room floor.

Another gift had not been completed before I was taken to the hospital. It was to have been a doll house. I had scrounged an old carton for the purpose and begged two pages from a book of wallpaper samples a neighbor, for some unknown reason, had brought with her into camp. These, with the aid of scissors and dabs of wheat-paste, were to have been fashioned into an exquisite doll mansion. It wasn't finished, but Sandy loved it just the same.

"Okay, honey," Meredith said, "now come get your presents. Go on. Open them."

One by one I removed the sheets of notebook paper from my gifts: three implements—crude but, to me, beautiful.

"It's a kitchen set," Meredith explained. "How do you like it?"

Our "kitchen" consisted of a brick stove built in one tiny corner of Block 14–No. 7; the 9 x 12 room was "home" to the three of us. At night Meredith had surreptitiously wrested bricks from the rubble of an old wall the guards had torn down. The stovepipe had been patiently assembled from 21 old tin cans. The burner, the most difficult part to procure, was a thick metal tile form. For it we had paid the exorbitant price of two full cans of evaporated milk! But what a difference that "kitchen" made. During the winter we would take coal dust, mix it with clay, and make a kind of fuel. Then we would buy and cook a few items from the camp canteen, where a limited and odd assortment of food-stuffs were now and then sold. Thus we managed to supplement the wearisome half-palatable mess-hall diet which consisted mainly of fish soup, worm-ridden bread, eggplant, turnips, and a dark porridge made of "gaoling," a coarse grain used by Chinese to feed their swine. To this was sometimes added bits of pork and an occasional ration of one egg per person.

The first item of my "kitchen set" was a baking pan. (Not that anyone would ordinarily have succeeded in identifying it as such!) It had originally been an over-sized sardine can of the sort our White Russian neigh-bors sometimes received in packages. The rough edges had been lovingly smoothed and small handles had been fastened at each end. Now when our birthdays came and we got the usual two-cup ration of flour we could have ourselves a birthday cake!

The next implement was a spatula—made of real rubber. Meredith did not tell me until later that it had been carefully whittled from a discarded boot heel, a bonanza he had discovered in the camp trash heap.

Completing the set was a tea strainer. Afterwards I learned that the patch of screening from which the gift was devised was the remnant of a carefully scrubbed, well-boiled fly swatter!

My gift to Meredith was received with genuine amazement, and his delight repaid me many times over for my scheming.

The hour was over. Meredith had kissed me and rose to leave. Sandy flung her small arms around me.

"Mommy, Mommy, hurry up and get well so you can come back home," she said. Then they were gone.

Quietly I fingered the three objects on my bed. My kitchen set. My Christmas presents. Down the ward someone hummed, "Oh, come all ye faithful, joyful and triumphant. . . ." No carol had ever sounded sweeter.

We spent ten more months in the Wei Hsien compound, months that were the most difficult of my life. After a brief release from the hospital, I was returned to the same ward, this time because of typhoid. For 13 days I was semi-conscious, haunted by strange obsessions, my body covered by a tormenting rash.

Finally, on August 12, a mudball thrown over the camp wall concealed a note informing us that the war had ended. Five days later, U.S. paratroopers drifted into an adjacent field. With them came medicines, food, and the end of our ordeal.

God has given us many blessed Christmases since that dark December day in Wei Hsien. But nothing we have ever received has been more precious than those crude gifts.

What made those inherently worthless bits of trash so inestimably dear to us? In the absence of material things, we compensated in the only way we could—by pouring our hearts into our gifts. Each of them, so painstakingly secured, so meticulously shaped, said, "I love you."

And this Christmas, when we gather around our ornamented tree, partially hidden by a small mountain of gaily wrapped parcels, we'll think back to Wei Hsien and try to remember . . . try to remember.

Christine Helsby

Christine Helsby wrote for inspirational magazines during the second half of the twentieth century.

Joseph Leininger Wheeler

CHRISTMAS AFTER
THE DARK TIME

This story reflects what life might be like during and after a Dark Time; it is not intended to depict end times. The reader will note that after the Dark Time passes, life continues to be extremely difficult because the world's infrastructure is gone, and rebuilding such a thing from scratch takes time—a lot of it!

*J*t was good to feel the weight of backpack and sleeping bag on his shoulders again. It had been barely six years, but it seemed far longer. Far, *far* longer—for this was no longer the same world.

It had not seemed possible that anything worse could happen than the horrific meltdown of the World Trade Center. For things had, ever so gradually, begun to get better. People began to invest again, create jobs again, travel again.

Then it happened. Around the world, terrorism on an undreamed-of scale brought global transportation to a dead halt. But even that paled in comparison to what followed: An extremely large meteor slammed into the earth at a disastrous angle, resulting in a global shift in crustal plate motion, which in turn set off a chain reaction of natural disasters. In the remotest part of Siberia, a volcano erupted; another volcano blew its top in Patagonia, followed by three more in the high Andes, then Mount Shasta in California and Mount Fuji in Japan. Not all at once, but sporadically during a six-month period, and accompanied by devastating earthquakes.

After three months of quiet, Krakatoa in Indonesia erupted in a performance comparable to that of 1883. During the following four years, volcanoes all across the globe exploded into action, spewing the earth's mantle into the atmosphere. It was as though the earth's crust had turned into a giant sieve (cracked open by earth-quakes, volcanoes blasting through like so many geysers). Geologists soon gave up trying to predict which would be next. All this turned day into night. Towering tidal waves reduced coastal and low-lying cities and towns into so much kindling. It was almost impossible to predict them because they rolled back and forth, thundering into each other, then reversing course. Everywhere there were wind-driven fires raging out of control. Hurricanes, typhoons, and tornadoes abounded, rains became torrential, and blizzards of unprecedented ferocity raged, paying no attention to traditional seasons. Truly, it seemed that the end of the world had come.

Cars stayed in their garages, trains in their stations, ships at their docks, airplanes on their airstrips. Without electricity, it became extremely difficult to cool or heat buildings, turn on appliances, move elevators, or operate street signals. Working and living in high-rise buildings ended. The public sewage system broke down and garbage pickups ceased. Widespread contamination of water followed. Without telephones, radio, television, computers, printing, telegraphing, postal service, FedEx, or UPS, effective communication became extremely difficult. Most machines were either neglected or abandoned, and those which remained outdoors rusted away. The system for drilling, refining, shipping, storing, marketing, and distributing petroleum broke down. The job market all but ceased to exist. Bartering replaced money.

Because nations, states, counties, provinces, and towns were all bankrupt, public servants no longer reported in. The banking system had collapsed and there was no one to call in loans. With no legal system to enforce anything, governing became almost impossible. Without police, National Guard, or armed forces, no one's life or property was safe.

It didn't take long for people to realize that cities were death traps, so streets were soon clogged with seas of humanity, each person carrying or pulling all that he or she considered valuable in the world, each hoping that somehow, somewhere, food, clean water, and shelter might be found. As they streamed out of the cities and spread out through the countryside, terrible things happened. Especially to farming families who dared to resist the demands of these famished invaders.

In earlier times, a subsistence level of life would have continued nevertheless—and it still did in underdeveloped parts of the world. But most people in industrialized nations had lost the ability to survive on their own: to grow their own food, weave their own fabric, make their own clothes, construct their own furniture and buildings, teach their own children, or protect their own families and communities. Somewhere along the way, men and women had divorced themselves from the earth itself. In good times, society had continued to function even though the job market had become more and more service-oriented. Not so now. Without producers, starvation and exposure to the elements were inevitable. Without weapons, ammunition, and the ability to use them effectively, no one was safe from predators.

Fear. Fear stalked the world in Brobdingnagian boots, the earth shuddering under each step.

And so it was that with the almost complete breakdown of all the basic building blocks of civilization, there remained but two foundations one could count on: God . . . and family. It is said that "there are no atheists in foxholes." Just so, on a planet that seemed to be self-destructing, God appeared to be mankind's sole hope. As for family, armed with water-stained road maps, people trudged to wherever it was members of their families last resided, in hopes of still finding them there. Those who found each other pooled their resources and parceled out their responsibilities. The oldest members of a given family (those who actually knew how to *do* things, *make* things, and *grow* things) mentored those who had never developed such skills.

God did not permit life to cease: Anemic-looking plants managed to eke out an existence in this pale twilight world. Furthermore, here and there pockets of sunlight broke through the ash-laden skies, making crop-growing possible. Nevertheless, billions of people died—many from starvation and untold millions from diseases such as tuberculosis and new strains of pneumonia and influenza.

John paused at the crest of a hill and wiped his forehead. He was tired and sweaty. The darkness was finally beginning to dissipate, and the sun was visible once more. Many had wondered if it would ever again hold center stage in the sky and had wept when they first saw it reappear.

John's thoughts whirled chaotically: *Oh Lord, what is it You want me to do? Only I am left alive out of all my family. Somehow, You've kept me alive during the Dark Time, for what reason I cannot even guess. I still don't know how to grow things, though I've learned a little about how to make things. Why You woke me in the middle of the night and told me to pack up and walk north, I do not know, but, obedient to Your command, here I am. And here's my compass.*

❆ ❆ ❆

Days and weeks passed, and still he plodded north, making fifteen miles on good days. From time to time, he'd stop at a farmhouse and ask for temporary work. Almost always he'd be welcomed in, but only as a guest. No one had a job. But he could help with the chores and share his hosts' simple fare, meager though it be. In the evenings, families would gather around and talk or sing. (Here his guitar was always welcome—he hadn't been able to leave it behind.)

After a day or two with each family, he'd shoulder his knapsack and sleeping bag one morning after breakfast and move on. North, always north, in response to the divine command.

A month passed, two, and now three; then he crossed the Canadian border. For a while, he feared he'd be stopped and sent back, but most of the Canadians he met were kind. Destitution knows no enemies or borders—he was welcome to share what they had.

Two more months passed, and nights became warmer: spring was in the air! One morning, somewhat apprehensively, he took stock: *Lord, I'm still heading straight north, but I'm getting a bit worried. Farmhouses are getting farther and farther apart. . . . Should I stop? Should I turn around? Did I miss my destination?*

There was no answer.

Next time he came to a farmhouse and was welcomed in, he found it even harder to move on. He asked his host this question: "I'm heading due north— been doing so for months now. If I keep going, what should I expect?"

The father of the family shook his head ominously. "Son, if I were you, I'd turn back. Before the Dark Time, things were different. But now, so many people have died that we know of only about a dozen families living north of us—after that, the wilderness. Once you enter that vast region, you'll be on your own. Do you have a gun?"

"Only a hunting pistol."

"Ammunition?"

"Still quite a bit."

"Good. You'll need it if you keep going!"

Several days later, he bade his adieus, walked out to the road, and headed north again. It took an entire day of fast walking before he reached the next farmhouse, but to his disappointment there was no one home. At the next one, another day north, the man who came to the door was rude to him. "We don't have food enough for ourselves, much less strangers!" he said, and slammed the door. Disconsolately, John hit the road once again, exhausted and hungrier than he'd been in a long time. It was two full days before he saw signs of another habitation. It was massive, constructed of giant logs, almost baronial, and looked like it had been there a long time. It was flanked by three huge trees, and one of Canada's greatest rivers looped around the largest barn he'd seen since crossing the Canadian border.

He reached the barn first, but seeing no one there, he continued on up to the big house, walked up onto a wide veranda, and, with some trepidation, knocked on the door.

A woman, perhaps in her forties, extremely attractive and young-looking still, opened the door. Seeing how dusty and exhausted he appeared to be, she welcomed him in . . . and he wondered if he'd suddenly been translated to heaven! The largest fireplace he'd ever seen outside a ski lodge dominated an extremely large open room. Stretching away in each direction were beautifully designed bookcases, overflowing with books that appeared to be both loved and read. Paintings by artists he knew graced the walls between bookcases and open windows. Comfortable sofas and chairs begging to be sat in were arranged artistically here and there. The vaulted ceiling was several stories high, one of the most beautiful he'd ever seen. The room was lit by gas lamps, the crackling fire in the great fireplace, and the sun shining through the windows. And completing the vision was a nine-foot Steinway grand piano. Of all the houses he'd entered and left during the last six years, this was the first that seemed like the home he'd known before the Dark Time. There was peace here.

The woman of the house, interrupting his reverie, suggested he use the nearby bathroom and wash up, which he did. When he emerged, he walked back into the kitchen and said, "Ma'am, I'm amazed. First hot water I've touched in years!"

She smiled. "It is a near miracle, isn't it? It's because we have a natural gas well on the property. The house was hooked up to it some years ago. . . . We do get spoiled with it. . . . By the way, here are some cookies, hot out of the oven, and some cold milk. Supper will be ready in a couple of hours. Listen for the bell."

Resuming his seat by the fire, he lit into the cookies and milk. He hadn't realized before now how utterly famished he'd been. Then he put the tray down and leaned back. It was all more than his weary body could process; when the woman entered the room about an hour later, he'd fallen asleep. She smiled. "Poor boy! Must have come a long, long way!" Gently, she tucked a warm blanket around him and returned to her duties. Night came, the bell rang, supper was eaten, the dishes were washed and put away, three roguish faces peered down at the sleeper and moved on, the lamps were extinguished one by one, yet still he slept on.

He was awakened next morning by the sun shining in on him. Initially he had no idea where he was, but gradually awareness came to him. What that woman must think of him! Hearing someone puttering around in the kitchen, he stepped in and, red-facedly, apologized.

"Don't let that bother you a second, young man! Feel free to use the bathroom down the hall to the right. You can shave, shower, change, and feel prepared for this new day. Breakfast will be ready in about an hour. Listen for the bell."

Sometime later, hearing the bell, John found his way into the dining room—then stopped dead in his tracks. Already seated at the table were three of the prettiest girls he'd seen in a long time. Their merry eyes did little to ease his discomfiture: *What must they think about my rudeness of yesterday?*

The lady of the house took mercy on him, saying, "I think it's time for introductions: I'm Mary Westcott— most people call me 'Mother Mary.'" Turning to the three girls, she gazed fondly at them a moment, then said, "As for my daughters, I'll let each one introduce herself."

Faith introduced herself first, followed by Hope, and

last of all Charity. Then it was his turn: "I'm John LaSalle, once of New Orleans, Louisiana. But that was before the Dark Time."

He took his seat by the youngest (and loveliest) of the three, Charity, and found himself strangely tongue-tied. Mother Mary reached for the hands of two of her daughters, and Charity's hand reached out for his. All bowed their heads as the mother prayed, "Oh Lord, in the stillness of this beautiful morning, we thank You for the gift of food, the gift of life, the gift of family, the gift of sunshine, and the gift of friendship. Especially we ask that You will bless our association with John today. . . . In His name, Amen."

Before breakfast was over, Mother Mary turned to John and asked, "John, what brings you up to this isolated part of the world?"

There followed a long pause as he struggled to find the right answer. Finally, after the silence became embarrassing, he decided to just tell the truth. After all, this family openly professed Christianity.

"Well, it was in response to an inner Voice that told me to pack my knapsack and begin walking north. That was over five months ago. But the Voice has not spoken to me since, so I have no idea how I'll know when I've reached the place God sent me to."

"If you keep walking north you realize, don't you, that the wilderness is no longer as easy to penetrate as it was before the Dark Time?"

He gulped. "I'm becoming aware of that."

"What kind of a timetable are you on?"

"I'm not."

"Would you be willing to stay here for a time and do some work for us before moving on?"

"I'd welcome the opportunity."

"Do you know much about farming?"

"No."

"Milking?"

"No."

"Horses?"

"Quite a bit. We used to have several."

"Yoking horses to things like a plow?"

"Oh, goodness no!"

"But you'd be willing to learn?"

"I've wanted to learn how for some time."

"Very well, we'll teach you. I don't mind telling you that you're an answer to prayer. Since we lost my husband, Reuben, and the girls' two brothers, Judah and Joseph, during the Dark Time, we've been very worried about how we'd get a crop in. Though we're able to keep up with our large garden and milk the few cows we have left, there's only so much of the heavy farm work we can do by ourselves. . . . Just consider yourself one of the family during your stay here, John. . . . Now, why don't you girls give John a tour of the place, show him where things are, and I'll do the dishes. . . . No, I mean it. Scat!"

❄ ❄ ❄

And so began his life as a northern farmer. He knew so little about the life that he was forever making mistakes. But all four women had a good sense of humor and merely laughed at his blunders. In only a few days, he felt he'd known them always. Faith, the oldest, was twenty-three. Tall and willowy, she was the most regal-looking of the three sisters, the wisest, and also the one who laughed least. It hadn't always been so, he learned. Benjamin, her childhood sweetheart and then fiancé, had died during the Dark Time. And with him, most of her dreams.

Hope, twenty-one, was the wittiest. If she wanted to, she could slice you into ribbons with her razor-sharp tongue. But she could be so funny, everyone forgave her for her occasional forays into sarcasm.

As for Charity, nineteen, she was beyond capsulizing. Far more than the sum total of fiery brunette hair, deep blue eyes, long eyelashes, captivating dimples, and tenderness. She was born with a deep love for every one of God's creatures and was forever bringing home animals or birds that had been wounded, crippled, or abandoned.

John found that his biggest challenge, as he'd feared, was learning how to handle the big Belgian draft horses, Sam and Dan. He could well understand why in medieval times their ancestors, the old Flemish heavy horses, were used as chargers by knights. Sam and Dan were deep-chested and massive, each weighing well over 2,500 pounds, and there wasn't much they couldn't pull if they had a mind to.

Ah, that was the rub! *If* they had a mind to. John was sure for weeks that the horses were laughing at him behind his back. It was some time before they took him seriously.

Sam and Dan had been born the same spring twelve years ago, and they were inseparable. It was unthinkable to yoke up one without the other! Had he tried to, the yoked one would not have moved an inch. Dan was the sly one, the most mischievous. After he'd pulled a load for a while, he'd get bored, glance back to see if he was being watched, then give Sam a quick nip. Sam would rear and thrash about; it would be only with great difficulty that John could regain control. All the while, Dan would look *so* innocent and eye Sam reproachfully, as if to say, *Why, you cantankerous hunk of misbegotten horse-flesh, why can't you behave yourself and be a model citizen like me?* Sam would just take it and look at John with a martyr expression that spoke volumes: *If you only knew the troubles I have to bear! That no-good Dan—sometimes I'd like to kick him into the next province. He nips me so hard, so often, and so sneakily, then has the gall to put on his Mr. Innocent sideshow!*

Once only, John saw long-suffering Sam get revenge. After a particularly savage nip, the end of the workday finally came. John unharnessed Dan first, dropped the harness on the ground some fifteen feet back, then proceeded to unharness Sam. Immediately afterwards, after first glancing backwards, Sam backed up to where Dan's harness lay, then generously pooped all over it.

How the family roared when John told the story at the supper table. The matriarch wiped her eyes and said, "You know, those Belgian draft horses yoke for life. My father had a pair—ours are of the same stock: Abe and Ishmael. Abe lived until thirty-two years of age; when he died, it broke Ishmael's heart. He gave up on life, refused to eat or drink, and one morning they found his cold and lifeless body on the barn floor."

Beside the Belgians, there were also three Arabians:

Sultan, Sultana, and Vizier—all that were left of the original nine.

Mother Mary began each day by reading a biblical passage. Supper was always special. Partway through, Mother Mary would look around the table and say, "Tell us, each of you, about your day. What was the happiest moment? Was there a sad one too?" John learned a lot about each daughter by their responses to these nightly questions. Faith's answers were the most insightful, Hope's the most lighthearted, and Charity's the most tender.

Since the nearest farm was five miles away, the family lived pretty much to themselves. During the Dark Time, very little association with neighbors had taken place. Had this not been so, the girls, each so attractive in her own way, would most likely all have been married or engaged by now. As it was, John would sometimes catch them with pensive faraway looks in their eyes, and sighs when they thought they were alone. Consequently, they each took more than a normal interest in this young man who had so unex-pectedly, and providentially, landed in their midst. They all liked him, that was soon clear. They also admired him because he got up each time he fell down (which was often!) and tried not to make the same mistake twice. His laugh was infectious; in fact, Mother Mary said one evening at the dinner table, "John, you'll never know how much happiness you've brought into this house." Then she winced, and John realized, *She's thinking about what it will be like when the planting is all done and I walk north again.*

One afternoon, in the midst of plowing, John had a

sudden conviction, as clear as though a voice had spoken to him out loud: "Stop work immediately and go to the house!" After hobbling Dan and Sam, he took off for the house at a lope. Seeing a strange horse tied to a post next to the house, he began to run. Up the steps and into the big kitchen he ran, and found standing there a tall man with a weak chin. John took an instant dislike to him. Moments later, he realized that this was the neighbor who had slammed the door on him several months earlier.

The man apparently had been threatening the four women, for there was a strained look on each of their faces. Mother Mary spoke in an icy tone John had never heard before: "Mr. Coleman, here is the master of this house. Tell him what you're here for."

The stranger took in the powerful build of his evident antagonist, noted the steely glint in the greenish-brown eyes, and began to mumble words that were almost inaudible, including something that sounded like "Musta made a mistake," and began backing toward the door. Gaining the porch, he almost ran for his horse. John followed him. Grasping the horse's reins in his right hand, John warned the intruder, "Never step foot on this property again!" then let go of the reins. Instantly, Coleman wheeled his horse and galloped away.

Hurrying back inside, John confronted the four women. "What was all that about?" he asked. All four answered at once. John smiled. "One at a time, please."

Faith looked at the others, then turned to him. "John, Mr. Coleman is an evil man. As long as Dad and our brothers were here, he didn't dare come on our property, for we all knew what kind of man he was. The whole province does! But now that he assumed we were unprotected, he rode up and—" her face blanched— "and he told us in no uncertain words that if we didn't . . . uh . . . give him what he wanted, terrible things would happen to us. 'After all,' he snarled, 'there's no one close enough to protect you!' Then *you* walked in."

John walked over to his favorite armchair and almost fell into it: *What had he let himself into?* He turned to Mother Mary. Reading his mind, she said, "'Master of this house'? It was our only hope! And it did catch him off guard. He'll now be making inquiries about you. Mark my words, John, he'll stop at nothing to get rid of you. Perhaps for your safety," and there was maternal solicitude in her eyes, "it's time for you to move on."

Instantly he retorted, "*Then* what would happen to you?"

No one replied, but their faces gave him his answer.

He got up from his chair and said, "I'm going to saddle Sultan and take a ride. I need time alone to think."

About thirty minutes later, at a rocking gallop, he saw ahead of him the blue waters of Half Moon Lake, so named because of its crescent shape. Reaching its edge, he dismounted and tied the Arabian to a tree.

Walking over to his favorite rock, he sat down on it and stared out across the blue water with unseeing eyes. *Dear Lord,* he began, *You sent me north but never told me where I was supposed to stop. So I'm in a quandary. Is this the place where You need me most, or does someone else, further on, need me more? But if I do go, who will protect these women, so isolated, so alone? Tell me, please, Lord.*

No answer came. About an hour later, he sensed a sudden coolness; looking up, he saw ominous clouds—a storm was coming! It hit just as he reached the gate to the outer corral. He rubbed Sultan down and put the tack away. He was drenched by the time he reached the house steps. But just before he took that first step, the Voice spoke to him—the same Voice that had sent him on this journey:

Who do you think it was that ordered you to stop plowing and go immediately to the house?

A chill not of the storm swept through him, and he dropped on his knees in the pouring rain. Lifting his face heavenward, he looked up and said, "Thank you, Lord. Thank you!" Then he got up and walked into the house.

They were all waiting for him. It was Charity who rushed up to him and said, "Oh, John, we were so worried about you, caught up in this storm!" Then, blushing crimson, she returned to her place by the fire. The others laughed; only Mother Mary remained unsmiling, searching his face. He drew near to her and, gently taking her hands into his, said solemnly, "This afternoon, God told me to stop my plowing and rush to the house—oh, goodness! Dan and Sam are still out there!" He rushed out the door into the intensifying storm. He found the horses, trembling with fear at the thunder and lightning strikes, then led them to the safety of the barn.

Next day, he unlocked the gun cabinet, selected the most powerful rifle, cleaned and oiled it, then began practicing. Fortunately, there were plenty of bullets available.

The women said nothing, only looked at each other knowingly.

The rains came again and again, and the crops grew and flourished.

Harvesttime came, and soon the granaries were full. Day after day, John smelled the sweet fragrance of fruit being canned by the four women. Then he helped them haul the jars down into the large storage-house deep underground where it was always cool.

One morning, a carriage drawn by four horses drew up to the house. "Oh, it's our neighbors, the Burne-Joneses!" shouted Hope. "Haven't seen them in ever so long!"

A man, a woman, and two daughters in their early twenties got out and were welcomed in like long-lost relatives. Everyone seemed to be talking at once. Since the seven women ensconced themselves in the parlor, John was left to entertain the man. William was his name. They were soon talking as though they had always known each other.

After a time, John asked, "You know, we're so isolated here that we've lost all contact with the outside world. What's happening out there?"

"My, you *are* isolated," William said. "We're only five miles from you, yet we've managed to keep up—at least somewhat—with what's happening. Granted, it's tough to. What we *do* pick up is generally by word of mouth. . . . But, in answer to your question, the great world out there is slowly, very slowly, coming to life again."

"The U.S., too?"

"Yes, the U.S., too. . . . But *everything* is having to be rebuilt. And priorities are different from what they were before the Dark Time."

"How so?"

"Well, first of all, people realize that God has been their only constant; only He has carried them through. And they're scared to death that, without His protecting hand, the volcanoes will begin erupting again."

"I wonder if that's true just for North America, or is it true for other continents as well?"

"Interestingly enough, John, a couple of weeks ago I actually rubbed shoulders with a continental traveler."

"Thought the species was extinct," quipped John.

"Not quite. It turns out that some of the old sailing vessels—including, of all things, windjammers!—are seeing active duty carrying passengers to other continents. Well, this traveler—a Mr. Farrell, I believe—had just returned from Europe."

"Things any better there?"

"No. Same as here. But one thing he said really struck home. You're aware, I assume, that before the Dark Time, Europe had become almost completely secular?"

"That's an understatement, William. Last figures I had, only 2 percent of Europeans attended church anymore."

"Well, you'll find his report hard to believe then. He told me that the churches and cathedrals of Europe are filled to overflowing: not enough room for all who want in."

"Unbelievable! God does work in mysterious ways. . . . I hope you don't mind my questions, but I'm so starved for information. . . ."

"No problem at all. Fire away."

"What else is happening?"

"Significantly, there's been a return to family, the only thing other than God we can count on in this thing called life."

"How true! What else?"

"You'll be most interested in this: People everywhere have rediscovered the land and are in no hurry to return to cities. Of course, cities are still a long way from being ready to receive them; the infrastructure of the entire world is being reconstructed."

"Where's the money coming from?"

"Good question. It isn't. Taxes come from salaries, and salaries are still virtually nonexistent. But there are interesting developments."

"How so?"

"Well, during the Dark Time, people began to make things again. As a result, craftsmanship is coming back."

"You don't say!"

"I do indeed. Down the road a ways, I see factories springing up, factories where things are created and built. No one talks much anymore about returning to a service economy, with most everything built overseas."

"About time!"

"True. And, you know, John, people have rediscovered silence . . . and serenity . . . and are mighty reluctant to return to all that noise. Same for advertising.

What's scaring former media moguls to death is that almost no one wants to see them come back."

"They certainly don't have *my* vote."

"Strange as it may seem, survivors are now saying that they've never in their lives been as happy, and as at peace with God and themselves, as they've been since the advent of the Dark Time. That the so-called 'Dark Time' was, in truth, the very best time they'd ever known, for it saved them and their families from being destroyed by the truly Dark Power."

John shuddered. "We had evidence here of that Dark Power not too long ago."

"Coleman?"

John nodded.

"Not surprised. He's been making inquiries about you. Means you no good."

"Nor does he mean good for the four Westcott women."

"I've no doubt of that, and neither do our friends."

"I've been practicing with the Remington every day."

"You're a wise man. How good are you at it?"

"Better than I ever thought I could be. As for ammunition, there's lots of it stored away here. It's almost like Reuben and his sons knew what was coming, and hence stockpiled a veritable arsenal."

"Reuben was one of the wisest men I've ever known. He did the same with food. He and the boys dug a deep icehouse so that food could be preserved almost indefinitely, even without electricity. Did the same thing beneath the barn to preserve food for the horses and cows."

"I've always wondered how those underground storehouses came about."

"The Westcotts have kept mum about this, for obvious reasons. During the Dark Time, people killed for far less. . . . Reuben buried kerosene in large underground tanks. Also had a thing about precious metals. Kept telling me the day was coming when money wouldn't be worth the paper it was printed on. And that was before terrorists destroyed the way of life we once knew. So he stockpiled gold and silver too. Now, of course, in the absence of paper money, gold, silver, and precious stones have once again become the unofficial currency of the world. Krugerrands and American Eagles have left their vaults and are circulating in the place of currencies. Mines are reopening and being worked everywhere."

"So what killed Reuben and the boys? No one here ever talks about it."

"Not surprised. Deep in one of their wilderness holdings—you're aware, aren't you, that their holdings are vast?—there was one of those strange and miraculous things we called 'pockets of sunlight,' which made limited crop-growing possible. Periodically, Reuben and the boys would travel up there to cultivate crops. Somehow, word got out, and the three of them were gunned down during one of their harvests."

"Oh no!"

"Oh yes. It was the saddest thing! Ironically, though, the murderers were caught in a blizzard. Froze to death with the cart of food they killed for. It was almost a month before the women found out what happened—then, this house was like a tomb for a long time."

There was a long silence while John digested that

horror. Then he continued his questioning: "I'm also curious, William, what's happening school-wise?"

"Not much. The entire world has been homeschooling for—let's see, going on six years now, and families have never been closer. Nor kids more motivated to learn. I'm guessing it'll be a long time before formal schools return."

"And government?"

"Virtually nonexistent. Takes taxes to run one, and we're still a long ways from being able to pay them. Why, we're still on a barter economy and are likely to remain so for a long time to come. The only government that exists is pro bono and local."

"So without police protection, is crime likely to return, like it did during the Dark Time?"

"You said it, brother. That's why we came over. . . . What do you say we go join the ladies?"

❊ ❊ ❊

When all nine had found seats in the Great Room, William tapped his armchair for attention. Instantly, there was absolute silence. After establishing eye contact with each person, he cleared his throat and began to speak: "I've been talking with John for some time now—it's my conviction that he's a godsend."

Murmurs of agreement arose.

"I've updated him on what's happening in the great world out there. He'll fill you in after we leave. But I have additional news, and I'm afraid it's not good."

"Oh no!" groaned Mother Mary.

"But, dear friends, it could have been far worse. We

could have gotten here too late—not just for you but for us as well."

"How is that?" asked Faith.

"Hear me out. As you're aware, during the Dark Time, all law and order broke down. And, just before the end of it, three of your family were victims of that anarchy. With the return of sunlight, there was so much euphoria that we've had a number of months of peace. Sadly, that peace is coming to an end."

"Why?" asked Charity, almost in a whisper.

"Oh, for a number of reasons. But the primary one is this: In the absence of a government or a police force, Canada is frontier once again. And what was the frontier like, John?"

After a pause to think out the question, John answered: "In order to preserve society, their property, and the lives of those they loved, people banded together for protection. Since might made right, they made sure there was as much might in every ranch, hamlet, or community as they could possibly scrape together."

"Precisely. That is happening even as we speak. Coleman and his henchmen are planning surprise attacks on places they deem most isolated, and hence most vulnerable."

Mother Mary's face turned ashen.

"Tell them about the meeting, Bill," broke in his wife.

"Oh yes. Secretly, the law-abiding leaders of our region got together last night at our house. Ostensibly, it was to celebrate my birthday. In reality, it was to organize a counterforce to lawless elements that are gathering strength. At the end of the meeting, yours truly was chosen sheriff of this region."

Enthusiastic applause!

"Not so fast. It's not so much an honor as a grave responsibility. Even though I'll be serving the entire region, the households most at risk are the seven of us bordering the wilderness. Thus we concluded that we had not a moment to lose. That's why we're here. John, I hereby appoint you one of my associate sheriffs, your word being law in my absence." John sat up straighter and grew even more serious.

"As you know, the seven households that border the wilderness got together early in the Dark Time and came up with a mutual defense system: if one of us was attacked, the others would come to our aid."

"But we never had to use it," pointed out Faith.

"And we may not have to now, but the way things are going, I'll be surprised if we don't. Mary, is your underground natural gas system still operating well?"

She nodded.

"Before sundown every night, I want you to light the gas torches Reuben placed strategically around the house. Extinguish them each morning. Hope, do you still have your pigeons?"

"Why, yes."

"Good." Turning to his daughter Isabel, he said, "The Westcotts know how our pigeon plan worked, but I doubt John does."

"You're right there," said John. "Please explain."

A bit flustered about being so suddenly put on the spot, Isabel said, "Well, it's this way. Homing pigeons only 'fly home' in one direction. So each ranch has trained a number of pigeons. Periodically, we get together to 'trade' so that we all have pigeons trained to fly to each of the other ranches. If you need us to come running, release pigeons belonging to each ranch, and thus each household will be alerted about the same time. When a pigeon flies through a special entry near a designated window, a little bell will ring and awaken the occupant of that room."

Curious, John asked, "How do we know whose pigeons are whose?"

"Oh, sorry! Should have explained that: each household was assigned a certain color. When the birds were young each was fitted with a leg band in the color representing its home of origin."

Now William stepped in again. "I'm guessing that since we haven't used our pigeon warning system in some time, some practice drills may be necessary, so we have not a moment to lose. Let's get moving on that this very day.

"Mary, do you still have the huskies?"

"Yes."

"Are they as alert as they used to be?"

"Well, no. We didn't think we had to worry much about break-ins any more."

"Well, you do now. It's time to retrain them to bark at any foreign presence on your land, day *or* night.

"Good thing Reuben put on a metal roof during that tinder-dry period when we had so many forest fires. But that still leaves the wooden walls. Still have that underground pipeline coming down from the big spring on Pilot Hill?"

"Yes, it keeps our water storage tanks full and gives us water pressure."

"Good! We may need to access those tanks in case they try to set this house on fire."

At sight of their stricken faces, he smiled and said, "I'm hoping all this, too, is merely precautionary and won't ever be needed. But we *must* be prepared!

"John, strengthen *all* the outside doors so they can't be battered down so easily. Also, it will be your duty to round up the emergency shutters Reuben made and reattach them. In case of attack, they can be hand-cranked closed from inside, leaving only small openings for rifle barrels. Yes, rifle barrels. It will also be your assigned duty to practice with the family every day. You have plenty of ammunition, so don't spare it as you practice to improve your marksmanship. If you ever do have to use rifles in an actual attack, first shoot only to scare the invaders off. If that doesn't work, shoot low to wound only. Hope that we never get to a life-or-death situation. Keep in mind that each of the women in the other ranches will practice their marksmanship every day as well. That's the way it used to be on the frontier, you know.

"Now, let's do a trial run. What do you do if the dogs begin to bark some night, and you see by the outdoor gas torches that you're being attacked?"

"First of all, crank in the shutters," volunteered Faith.

"Next, retrieve the rifles from the gun cabinets and begin firing, but close to, rather than at, attackers," said John.

"And unleash the pigeons," said Hope.

"And if John is away?"

"We hold the fort anyway," said Charity bravely.

"By the way, John, if pigeons from one of the other ranches fly through the special opening in Hope's room, it will be your duty to quickly dress, arm yourself, saddle up, and immediately rush to that household's aid."

"Back to us. What if, in spite of everything we do, the attackers break through? What then?" asked Faith, clearly worried.

"Then it's your exit of last resort, designed and constructed during the Dark Time: the secret passageway which permits you to escape the house and get to the outer barn where the horses are stabled. Then ride away! No loss of mere possessions could possibly compensate for the loss of any of our lives!"

After considerable additional discussion, including a fairly long one between Hope and Isabel, the meeting broke up. The guests climbed back into their carriage and were borne homeward by the four dappled gray horses.

❄ ❄ ❄

Next morning at the breakfast table, Mother Mary opened her Bible to Psalm 91 and began to read:

> "He that dwelleth in the secret place of the most High shall abide under the shadow of the Almighty. I will say of the Lord, He is my refuge and my fortress: my God; in him will I trust."

Lines followed that believers have gone to for courage ever since they were first written:

"He shall cover thee with his feathers, and under his wings shalt thou trust. . . . Thou shalt not be afraid for the terror by night; nor for the arrow that flieth by day. . . . A thousand shall fall at thy side, and ten thousand at thy right hand; but it shall not come nigh thee. . . . There shall no evil befall thee. . . . For he shall give his angels charge over thee, to keep thee in all thy ways."

Then she looked up, smiled, and said, "In all our preparation for what may never come, let us not forget Who rules the universe still. Be of good courage: the Lord has always carried us through before, and He will do so again. Let us pray."

❋ ❋ ❋

As day followed day, and no intruders disturbed their nights, they began to relax a little. It was good to be in regular contact with neighbors again, and during the practice drills, the pigeons faithfully carried messages back and forth.

One balmy October day, John saddled up Sultan and cantered off for a ride. As he approached his favorite Eden on the ranch, Half Moon Lake, he noticed a tethered horse and a familiar figure on "his" rock. His heart began to race. After tethering Sultan near Sultana, John walked over toward Charity, surprising her out of a reverie.

She smiled up at him. "Oh, it's *you.*"

"Is that bad?" he teased.

"No, not at all." She seemed at a loss for words.

He changed the subject. "So you like it here too?"

"I've always loved it," she said so softly he had to bend his ear to hear her. "It's my favorite dreaming place."

"And what dreams have you dreamed here?"

She blushed. "That would be *telling.*"

"Oh?"

"But I can tell you about *one* of them."

"Please do!"

"Up on that rise, near that clump of evergreens, is where I've always wanted to build our house."

"*Our* house?" he questioned impishly.

"Naughty boy! *My* house, then."

"So what would you like *your* house to be like?"

"Oh, that's easy!" Her eyes sparkled. "A log cabin. Not too big, not too small, but a *big* fireplace, a cute little kitchen, a wide porch so we—I mean *I*—can watch the animals and birds who love it here too, and the sunsets and the storms and the seasons. And of course there would be . . ." She stopped in confusion.

He didn't spare her: "You weren't, by chance, going to add a 'he' and perhaps even a family?"

She looked at him intently for a moment, trying to find out if he was making fun of her. Then she proceeded, "Well, yes, it's entirely *possible*—but not *probable* (we're so isolated here) that there might some-day be a he."

"What would he be like?"

She looked at her watch in apparent dismay. "Oh! It's getting late—Mom will need me to help fix supper!" Quickly she stood to her feet and shook free her long gold-burnished brunette hair.

He helped her mount Sultana and watched her ride away with ne'er a look back—well, once, when she thought he couldn't see her glance back over her shoulder.

❆ ❆ ❆

After supper one evening, Mother Mary turned to John with an air of purpose and said, "John, you've told us already a little bit about your earlier life. Now that the world is, ever so gradually, beginning to wake up again, have you given much thought to what you'd like to do with the rest of your life?" Instinctively, John sensed that the question, ostensibly a casual one, was in reality anything but. All three girls leaned forward a bit to catch his answer, but he had eyes for only one. Several times he'd asked himself this question: *Why is it when there are three young women to choose from, almost equally attractive, that there is virtually no contest? All I know is that whenever I look at Charity, I melt.*

"We-ll," he stammered, trying to buy time, "before the Dark Time, I was interested mainly in just having a good time and getting high enough grades so I wouldn't flunk out and embarrass my folks." Charity's lips set in a severe line: clearly, she'd expected better of him. He gulped. There was a long silence while he searched for the right words to say. "But then came the Dark Time, during which I lost my father, my mother, and my sister, Jane."

The hard set of Charity's lips softened a bit.

"During the rest of the Dark Time—like most folks—I just tried to stay alive, doing whatever odd jobs

I could find in return for food. Our money—once upon a time Dad had lots of it—was worthless, little better than Monopoly money. . . . Then the dark began to break up, the Voice spoke, and I headed north."

Again, there was a long silence as he searched for the right words to bridge with. "Well, then I came here—this place I've come to love." Charity looked away. "I also need to tell you that during the Dark Time, God came back into my life. After Dad and Mom died"—and he struggled for composure—"I was left with nothing—no one, but God. . . . Then I came here, and it was like I'd found home again. You became the family I lost. So much so that I'd consider it the greatest gift imaginable if—if you don't want to get rid of me." *There, it was out in the open.*

Charity now looked up, and her clear eyes met his. "John," and her saying his name was like a caress, "I'm curious about something: that Voice you said sent you here. Do you by any chance remember about when it was?"

"As a matter of fact, I do. It was the day after my birthday, early in the morning of November 3."

"Excuse me!" Charity left the table and hurried out to the kitchen. After rummaging around in several drawers, she returned with a large calendar and quickly turned the pages to November. Then, triumphantly, she showed everyone two lines in Mother Mary's flowing script and read them out loud. "Entry for November 2: 'Tonight, at evening worship, we began praying that God would send someone soon who would help us save the ranch. We vowed to keep praying until that someone came.'"

"And," added Faith, "we prayed that prayer every day until the day you came."

There followed an almost eerie silence, as everyone sensed such a closeness to God they could almost feel angel wings.

After prayers were said and the girls had kissed their mother and retired for the night, Mother Mary turned to John and said with a smile, "What you said tonight touched my mothering heart. But John, I wasn't born yesterday. There was something—something very big—that you didn't say."

"What do you mean?"

"I don't think I have to tell you, John."

He squirmed uncomfortably, then said, "Well, there *is* something else: I love one of your daughters."

"No news to me," she answered.

His eyes widened. "Have I been that obvious?"

She half stifled a laugh, then said, "John, it was clear to this mother that since the very first moment you set eyes on my daughters, you had eyes for just one."

"I didn't know it showed."

"Mothers instinctively *know* things like that. It's what we're born for." Then she grew serious. "Charity's different from her sisters."

"I know."

"Perhaps you do, in part. But let me tell you, she's always been the most vulnerable one. Because she loves with her entire heart, she will love but once. . . . And if that one should happen to hurt her, or reject her, she will die inside. That lovely flower of joy will wither and all the lights will go out in her eyes."

His eyes met the mother's and held so that she read

his very soul. After a long silence, she asked, "John, how serious is it with you?"

Without hesitation he shot back, "She is the only woman for me—if she rejects me, there will never be another."

"As serious as all that?"

"As serious as all that."

Then she changed the subject again.

"But John, you realize that, according to the standards of the world you come from, she's somewhat naive."

She paused, then continued, "The man who truly loves and values her will court her at a very slow pace."

"I'm willing to do that."

"I wonder if you really are. I want all three of my girls to be virgins when they marry. And I hope and pray that condition will be mutual with the men they marry."

Again he looked her straight in the eye. "It would be so with me."

She relaxed a little, then added, "All right, you have my permission to court her."

He couldn't help asking, "Does she love *me?*"

The mother looked long and searchingly back at him before she answered, "I'm afraid you'll just have to find out for yourself, John. Besides, you might not value what comes to you too easily. But I must have your word that, generally speaking (with only rare exceptions), you'll court her only in our presence. I know how quickly raging hormones can trample on reason when you're young. Do I have your word, John?"

"You have my word."

"Good. I accept it. Now it's time to get some sleep."

"Good night, Mother Mary."

❊ ❊ ❊

Very early the next morning, Mother Mary knocked gently on her youngest daughter's door. A sleepy voice answered, "Y-e-s?"

"It's Mom."

"Oh! Come in!"

Opening it, the mother found her youngest, even with cobwebby eyes and tangled hair, to be so lovely she wondered how she could have given birth to her. She walked over to her bed and Charity opened her arms for the morning hug. After being held a few moments, Charity sat up, sensing something different: "Mom, what *is* it?"

There was a long pause before she answered. Finally, she said, "John has asked permission to court you."

The glow in Charity's eyes was almost blinding as she murmured, "I'm . . . *so* . . . glad!"

The mother asked a needless question. "Do you love him?"

Charity stared at her mother in disbelief, as though her mother had asked her, "Do you believe in God?" Then she answered passionately, "Of *course* I love him! I've loved him ever since I first saw him sleeping by the fireplace."

The mother sighed. "Do you know what 'courting' means?"

"Of course! Do you think I'm still a child? It means he wants to single me out, to spend more time with me than he does with Faith and Hope, talk to me more, and, and maybe," and here her voice stumbled.

"Yes, dear, it does mean all that—but what else?"

Charity stiffened and gently pushed her mother far enough back so she could read her eyes. "Mommy," (it had been *so* long since she'd used that childish term of endearment) "it also means that I don't have much time left in which to be a girl. . . . It means that he *may* ask— if he still loves me after—" She paused, her eyes registering a jolting discovery. "You haven't said that he loves me."

It was perhaps the hardest thing Mother Mary had ever done to avoid setting her child's heart at ease by saying, *Of course he does, dear! How could you doubt it?* Instead she said, tenderly, "I don't think it's my place to tell you that. In his own time, if it's there, it will be *his* place to tell you."

Charity's eyes lost their glow. *"If?"*

Again, Mother Mary had to struggle mightily with the temptation to remove that doubt. Finally winning out, she said slowly, choosing each word with extreme care, "Love is one . . . of the most complex things in the world."

Charity flared up indignantly. "How can it be complex? Either he loves me or he doesn't."

Mother Mary began to feel the earth giving way beneath her feet. Even more slowly, she said, "Please hear me out, dear. I asked you a question: What else?"

Quicksilverish thoughts raced through Charity's head, and the mother studied the blur—like fast-forwarded film. Finally, Charity answered, but now in a rather flat voice, with all joy gone. "It may also mean that he'll want me to marry him—and that would mean I'd have to follow him if he decided to leave our ranch."

Mother Mary probed again, "What else, dear?"

Suddenly, Charity blushed as a new thought came to her, one she'd never entertained before. "You mean, uh, it might mean—I mean, of *course* it would mean—" but she couldn't say it.

"Yes, Charity, it *would* mean that. Marriage brings with it joy and pain, just as life itself does. And emotional, spiritual, and physical intimacy brings both. If you are blessed, as I've been, it will also bring children—and they are born in pain. And you will suffer pain—empathetically—with each child as long as you live."

Gone was much of the girl in Charity's face: life was turning serious. "I see what you mean, Mommy. It's—it's not really simple at all, is it?"

Her mother could only nod, her heart aching for this youngest child.

Charity spoke again. "Is life always this, uh, this uncertain?"

"Yes, dear. Uncertainty is its name. Nothing is certain but God."

"Even John?"

"Even John. Even Charity. *Especially* courtship."

"How is that?"

"Well, you see, dear, men are strange animals."

"I know that!" retorted Charity.

"I wonder if you really do, dear. . . . They are born with strange quirks—we have them too."

"Like what?"

"Well, for one, they never seem to really value that which comes to them too easily."

Charity's face was a study. "So *that's* what all this has been about! Why didn't you tell me before?" A slightly impish glint came into her eyes. "Keep him guessing, make him work for me, don't let him know I'm so utterly in love with him that my temperature rises every time he's in the room . . ."

"Yes, darling. That's what I meant to say."

"Well, I can play that game." But again came an abrupt change of mood. In almost a wail, she said, "But I *don't want* to play that game! I'm not catty, I'm not a coquette, I'm not devious. In fact, he may think I'm simple compared to Hope and Faith."

"I know, dear. But you are not simple; you are steadfast."

"Oh, Mother, I can play the game—if I have to—if only . . ."

"If only what, dear?"

She crawled back into her mother's arms, hiding her crimson face on her mother's shoulder, her long gold-brown hair glorious in the dawn. Then in muffled tones came the pain-wracked words, "If only I knew for sure that he loved me."

Mother Mary thought, not for the first time, *How incredibly difficult is this thing called parenting! No one ever teaches you how to be a mother; you just stumble into it and hope you don't make a royal mess of it. . . . Reuben—oh Reuben, never have I needed your wisdom more than now! Reuben, how do I answer her? Life is so much more complex than I thought it would be when I was young—like Charity. Remember how adorable she was when she was a baby? She's*

always been adorable; don't know how any man could look at
her without falling in love with her. What do I say, Reuben?

In the end, she answered straight from her heart. Not
the sensible, rational, wise answer, but still the answer
she felt Reuben would have given to this daughter he
was always inwardly so partial to. Charity had owned
him since the very first time she lisped, "I lub you,
Daddy." Tightening her arms around Charity in an
embrace so tight it almost hurt, she said, "Yes, darling,
he loves you—how could he not?"

Charity pulled away, glory in the eyes of this girl-
woman. "Oh, Mommy! Oh, Mommy! Now I can play
the game." She chuckled, deliciously malicious. "Is that
poor boy going to have to work for me! In fact, I feel
sorry for him already."

Mother Mary laughed. "So do I, dear. So do I."

❋ ❋ ❋

And so the courtship began.

Each evening, during the music hour after worship,
John was as active a participant as the girls and their
mother. And often, when the instruments were put away
and the other sisters had immersed themselves in books,
John and his guitar would join Charity at the Steinway,
and they'd sing both their old favorites and learn new ones.

As often as possible, each morning they'd take a short
walk together. Yet, as the days and weeks passed, the
sisters became increasingly puzzled. One morning they
corralled Charity and Hope asked, "What's up, Char?
Poor John doesn't know if he's coming or going with
you—sometimes he looks befuddled. It's not like you,

for up till now you wore your heart on your sleeve for everyone to see."

Charity's laugh was a joy to hear: "You mean it's working? Oh, I'm so happy!"

Faith broke in, "*What's* working?"

Charity only looked wise and solemnly intoned, "Men do not appreciate what they get too easily."

The sisters collapsed in chairs and laughed until they cried. Hope finally regained her composure and said, "Oh, this is just too rich! But I sense a mother in this somewhere."

Charity merely put on her sphinx look.

❄ ❄ ❄

It had been so long since their neighbor's warning that they began to feel it might have been a false alarm. Nevertheless, John kept them at their firing practice and periodically put them through trial drills.

One dark September night, about two in the morning, the huskies began to bark. Not halfheartedly but with deadly meaning. Immediately, John leaped to his feet, lit a lamp, dressed, and raced down the hall to the Great Room. The women were already there, already dressed, ready for whatever might follow. The shutters were closed, followed by a brief prayer. Each of the five was sent to a window where they peered through the slits in the shutters. Positioned like this, each could command a view from a different side of the large house. For a time there was, except for the huskies, absolute silence. Then bullets began slamming into the front side of the house. John rushed down the hall to Hope. "The pigeons!" he called out.

"Will do!" she answered, then disappeared momentarily.

Shortly afterwards, as they peered out, they could see by the light of the torches at least a dozen attackers. John directed Mother Mary, Faith, and Hope to begin firing, but not *at* the figures. Charity was sent to the back side of the house to make sure the attackers didn't attempt to break in there.

It was so done, and rifle shots came perilously near the attackers.

Some time later, discomfited by the continual close calls, the attackers conferred together, then must have decided on a different plan of attack. They moved to the back of the house. John ordered a regrouping, and everyone joined Charity except for Mother Mary.

A little over an hour after the firing began, the besieged heard gunshots coming from other directions. Now the besiegers panicked and ran for their horses, only to discover, to their horror, that they were no longer there! The attack on the house ceased.

Some time later, there was a clatter of hoofs as William rode up to the front door. John went out to meet him. William rubbed his hands in delight. "We got 'em!" he chortled. "I believe we got 'em all. We came at them from all directions, firing just a tad over their heads or at their sides. They dropped their rifles and ran. Ran into the hands of the rest of our troop, who used the lasso to mighty good effect. They're in our custody now, and being marched—no horses for the likes of them!—to the old jail we haven't used in so many years. Within a few days, there'll be a trial. Old Henry Adams (used to be judge) will be temporarily reactivated. You and Mother Mary will be asked to testify."

"And Coleman?"

"If ever I saw a sheepish, craven-looking, green-faced ringleader, it was he! We surprised the socks off him and his gang! You'll inform the rest?"

"Of course!"

"Good. Gotta join the merry party. Tell Hope the pigeons worked great! Proof of which is, each of our six neighboring households are represented in our posse."

"Thank God you came that day, Will! I shudder to think where we'd be had this happened before we reactivated the mutual defense agreement."

"Yes. You've got *that* right: Thank God!"

"By the way, William, what happens if the judge convicts them?"

"Ever wonder why there were so many hangings on the frontier?"

"No. I just know there were a lot."

"It's because they couldn't afford to maintain jails. Hanging was a lot cheaper."

"So they all hang?"

"No. We'll give them an option: flee the country and live, or stay here and face the rope. I'm guessing they'll put on their traveling shoes."

And he wheeled his horse and rode away into the night.

※ ※ ※

Then came Christmas. John, having loved the season as a child, joyfully welcomed its coming. Gradually, the great house was readied for the season of the Christ Child.

Carol singing, Christmas storytelling, and reading took place every evening. As for gift-giving, so uncertain was John of Charity's love that he gave no sister a gift that might make the other two envious. As always, the Westcott family gifts were handmade.

So it was that Christmas Eve and Day came and went with no change in John's family status.

❄ ❄ ❄

On New Year's Day, Mother Mary called a family council. John was invited too. In fact, she asked him to offer a prayer for their new year.

Afterwards, she turned to John and said, "Son"—this was the first time she'd ever called him by that name— "I've talked this over with the girls, and we just don't feel it's fair for you to remain here under the current arrangement."

Everyone laughed at his woebegone expression. "Don't worry, John. It's not what you think. It hasn't escaped us that you've been carrying the weight of the entire ranch on your shoulders—and you haven't complained once. You've already told us that you lost your entire family. And the girls lost both father and brothers. You have already become," and here her voice broke, "more than a son to me. I've talked this over with the girls, and they urged me to move ahead. I'm having papers drawn up by Judge Adams to make you an equal heir with each of the girls to this property, which is larger than even you girls realize.

"It has remained intact for over three centuries and comprises some 300,000 acres." Everyone gasped. "But it is not a unit: much of it is in the Yukon and Northwest Territories, and is thereby preserved for all time for the Canadian people by our family. Not surprisingly, prior to the Dark Time our expenses and taxes were very large. That's why," and now she turned to John, "as the world began to creep back to normalcy, I began to fear for the future. Long ago, one of our ancestors purchased the estate from the king of France himself, and written into the deed are words to this effect, that Reuben long ago had me memorize: 'This estate will never be broken up, but will remain intact forever. It will remain the property of the entire family unless all the descendants should die.'" Then, turning to John, she continued, "Children by adoption will be considered equal heirs."

She then walked over to John and looked down at him with a face suffused with maternal love. "John, regardless of future events, regardless of matrimonial decisions you or any of my daughters"—and here she smiled at Charity, whose face was a study of conflicting emotions— "may make, from this day forth, you are my son, and you have sisters who already love you dearly.

"Welcome home, Son."

❊ ❊ ❊

The snows were beginning to melt away one balmy spring day when John asked Mother Mary if she had a moment.

"Of course! What is it, dear?"

He slumped down on the big leather sofa and sighed. "Oh, it's just that I never know where I am with Charity. Sometimes it seems that I'm making real headway; other times that I'm losing ground instead of gaining it. It's— it's downright discouraging. Sometimes—and oh how hard it is to say this!—I wonder if she really loves me!"

He didn't know what he expected to see in Mother Mary's eyes; he just wasn't expecting to hear her laugh. He looked up with a wounded expression and said, "I don't find that funny."

Mother Mary laid her hand on his arm, saying, "Forgive me, John. It's just that I'm not surprised by what you're saying. How long has it been since you began to court her?"

"Oh, about six months."

"And you expected immediate capitulation?"

A sheepish grin. "Well, sorta."

"You remember our earlier talk?"

"How could I forget it!"

"Would you have truly valued her love had it dropped into your hand like an overripe apple?"

Grinning, he answered, "Do I really have to answer that?"

"No. But do you see my point?"

"Y–e–s."

"John, let me ask *you* a question: Do you love her as much as you did when you started to court her?"

"Oh, much, much more! I love her more every day I'm with her. It's all I can do to avoid running away with her!" Then noting the look in her eye, he hastily amended, "But I promised."

"Yes, John, you promised, and I hold you to it."

"But Mother, sometimes I just don't know if I can stand the uncertainty any longer, the not knowing whether or not she even loves me. It's driving me crazy! If I just knew that deep down she loved me—even half as much as I love her—I think I could go on."

Again he was surprised at how unconcerned she appeared to be. Suddenly, he pounced: "Mother, you aren't being fair to me!"

"How so?" And still she smiled.

"You're holding back on me!"

"Oh?"

"Yes. You know more than you're letting on."

"Of course. Did you expect me not to?"

"No. It's just that, well, Jacob worked fourteen years for his Rachel, but at least he knew for sure that she loved him!"

"And you don't feel that Charity loves you?"

"Well, certainly as a sister, I do."

"But not more than that?"

"Sometimes I do, sometimes I don't."

"You're putting me in a hard spot, Son."

"I know, Mother. It's not fair, but you're my last hope—please don't let me down, *please!*" And his head fell onto her lap.

The mother ran her fingers through this new son's hair and mused, *How difficult it is to play God, to attempt to choreograph the lives of others. Have I really been fair to him? Have I?* She wrestled some time with this before she raised his head so she could meet his eyes.

"John, what possible reason do you have for demanding such an answer from me?"

"Because, Mother dear, I want to begin building a

house for her, for us, because I just can't live without her . . . not just as a sister but as my wife and lover, my soul mate, the mother of our children to come—" and then, slyly— "your grandchildren."

"You naughty, naughty boy!"

He just grinned.

"Where would you build it?"

"Above Half Moon Lake. It's the place we both love most!"

"When would you want to start?"

"Would today do?"

"Oh, my! Why do you make it so difficult?"

"Because I *love* her, Mother! And I know good and well you're holding out on me—and it isn't fair, me being your son—your only son."

That broke her. "Heaven forgive me for breaking a trust: Of *course* she loves you, John. Always has!"

"Really?" He leaped to his feet.

She nodded, smiling up at him.

"When could I start?"

"Any time."

"How could we keep Charity from riding over to the lake?"

"You leave that to me. I may not be very good at keeping secrets, but I ought to be able to handle *that.*"

His face radiant as it had not been in months, he grabbed her in a bear hug, practically squeezing the life out of her, and whirled her around and around the room while she laughingly begged him to let her down.

His only response was, "She loves me! She loves me! She loves me!"

Just then Charity stepped into the room, thoroughly confused. "She loves *what?*"

John released Mother Mary, his face frozen in a hand-caught-in-the-cookie-jar look, and fled.

Charity tried to be stern with her mother. "Mom, come clean. What have you two been up to?"

Mother Mary could hold it back no longer. She just laughed as she hadn't in a long time, and fled out the other door.

❊ ❊ ❊

"Mother—I'm concerned."

Whenever Charity *mothered,* something serious was up. "What's troubling you, dear?"

Leaning against the windowsill, Charity said, "It's John!"

"What's the matter—courtship not going well?"

"Oh, darn the stupid ol' courtship! I hate it! Wish I'd never agreed to play the game! Sometimes I wonder if I might not be losing him!" A tear trickled down her cheek.

"Why is that, dear?" her mother asked, trying to keep a straight face.

"Oh, sometimes he seems so distant, not ardent at all. And he's gone so much working on that project over by Half Moon Lake. Wish I hadn't promised not to ride over there any more!"

"But you gave me your word."

"Oh, I know I did. I'll keep it. It's just that I'm all mixed up. Nothing's working out right."

"Oh, I wouldn't worry too much about that."

"Mom," she coaxed, "you know something you're

not telling me. You're in collusion with that awful man—I just know you are!"

"Oh! So you don't love him anymore?"

"Mo–ther! Sometimes you're impossible!"

"Would it help for me to say you don't have anything to worry about?"

A strangling hug, a hundred kisses, and a joyful laugh she hadn't heard in weeks, was her reward.

What an old fool I am, mused the mother. *What an old fool.* But she smiled as she said it, and hummed an old English ballad, "Greensleeves," that Reuben had sung to her at their marriage ceremony. "Because," he had said, "you've always loved green, worn green, and green are your eyes, darling."

Autumn in the northern wilderness country had come again, more glorious than usual, it seemed to Charity. So in love, and determined not to show it. Too much, that is. Very early this morning, she had awakened engulfed by thoughts somersaulting through her dreams. After showering and putting on her favorite stonewashed jeans—how long she had made them last!—and shirt, she stole across the yard, through the trees, and down to the river (torrential in the spring but now languorous and tawny).

Always, as a girl, she'd had her favorite tree, a great river-loving willow—and her favorite perch was about halfway up. Dare she? In a fit of recklessness, she climbed up to it, leaned back, and waited for sunrise.

At first she thought it was part of the fabric of her dreams, so soft were the opening chords on a guitar.

But then came the words. The owner of the voice she knew!

So bewitching were her face and the long cascading burnished hair that the singer almost forgot Thomas Moore's lyrics to one of the most timeless of all Irish tunes:

> *Believe me, if all those enduring young charms*
> *Which I gaze on so fondly to-day,*
> *Were to change by to-morrow, and fleet in my arms,*
> *Like fairy gifts fading away,*
> *Thou wouldst still be adored, as this moment thou art,*
> *Let thy loveliness fade as it will,*
> *And round the dear ruin each wish of my heart*
> *Would entwine itself verdantly still.*

All the while, the guitarist looked up at the vision in the tree, his heart in both his eyes and his voice. Then came the second, one of the most treasured stanzas Western literature has ever known:

> *It is not while beauty and youth are thine own,*
> *And thy cheeks unprofan'd by a tear,*
> *That the fervor and faith of a soul can be known,*
> *To which time will but make thee more dear;*
> *No, the heart that has truly lov'd never forgets,*
> *But as truly loves on to the close,*
> *As the sun-flower turns on her god, when he sets,*
> *The same look which she turn'd when he rose!*

As he laid his guitar down, the fairy princess above said, in the tenderest tone she'd ever spoken to him, "I've always loved the words to that song."

"Which ones?"

"Well, pretty much all of them. The singer tells the woman that his love for her is not dependent on mere looks—for beauty never stays. But his love is built on something deeper. . . ."

"True. That's why I chose it. Every time you look in a mirror, you have to know you're beautiful. But there is a beauty deep inside you: a beauty of character, of heart, of spirit, of soul, that will endure—long after you and I are old. It is both types of beauty the song is about."

Then, with a roguish chuckle, she leaned down and said, "Like to climb trees?"

In an instant there he was, smiling across at her.

She patted the great limb she was perched on. "There's room for you here."

There was. To avoid falling, of course, his left arm had to enfold her, and her head found its home on his broad shoulder. The morning breeze tickled his cheeks with the tendrils of her long iridescent hair. Speech was not necessary, as it was one of those moments that are outside of time. They can never be past, present, or future—they just exist in movie-film three-dimensionality, those frames frozen forever. There were no more questions, no more answers—just the sacred moment.

Just before he released her, he gently kissed her hair and cheek, then helped her down the tree.

❄ ❄ ❄

She started the painting on a Monday some three weeks afterwards. It was not difficult to keep it secret, as each member of the family, after first shutting and locking their bedroom door (at some time during the day or evening), tackled mysterious things. For, even before the Dark Time, family tradition dictated that Christmas gifts had to be made or fashioned by hand rather than purchased in a store or by catalogue. These closed-door sessions became even more frequent as they entered the season of the Advent.

Up until that memorable riverside serenade, Charity had not known what to give John. Now that she knew, she could hardly contain her excitement. She was dissatisfied with her first two canvases, but the third was all she dreamed it could be. The presents for her sisters and mother were time-consuming too, but not like John's.

One reason there was such a close bond between the sisters and their mother was that she had homeschooled each of them during those crucial sail-setting early years. The family library had been growing over many generations, but it was Reuben who so dramatically expanded it. Whether it be a classic one was searching for, a book beloved by generations of families, a new book of real worth, biography, history, nature, science, religion, the arts, philosophy, resource material for research—you name it, you'd find it in the library.

Also, both parents insisted that each child learn to play the piano and at least one other instrument. And singing was part of their daily life. Thus they had enjoyed—up until they lost almost half their family—performing in their own choir and orchestra. They were also expected to develop to the fullest their other God-given talents.

John set up a towering white fir adjacent to the Steinway. The four women decorated it with ornaments they had crafted over the years, as well as those inherited from previous generations.

❋ ❋ ❋

Long ago, Mother Mary had begun a weekly tradition she never deviated from, not even during the Dark Time: Every Sunday morning, each child would find that a letter had been slipped under the door sometime during the night. The letters, having no particular pattern or subject matter, were geared to the individual needs of the recipient.

Early the first Sunday morning in December, Charity woke up and looked for her letter. After opening it, she took it over to her favorite rocker by the window and began to read.

> *My dearest Charity,*
>
> *How I wish your father were here to watch you blossom into the kind of woman we both hoped you would someday become. We were always such a team that I depended on him for half of the child-raising. Now I have to do it all alone, and I'm sure I botch up things he would have known how to deal with. You inherited so much of his sensitivity and love of beauty. He was so sentimental that he teared up during movies, reading some books or stories, or hearing certain pieces of music. I used to kid him about it, but it was one of the things I loved most about him. You have no idea how many times I've longed to see him sitting there by the fireplace—how he loved it!—reading a book, listening to music, or writing. Most of all I miss the love-light in his eyes when I'd*

walk into the room. I'd sometimes laugh at his romanti-
cism, his wild mood changes, his willingness to do crazy
things on a whim. I do believe that if I'd said one morn-
ing, "Reuben, let's drop everything and fly to Casa-
blanca" (or London or Rio or Jaipur or Bangkok or
Llasa), he'd have taken me in his arms, given me a
passionate kiss, and said, "Just us, or with the kids?"
And the next day, we'd have been on our way. Oh, how
I miss that! You have no idea how many times my
pillow's been stained with tears!

Charity lowered the letter. Curious how children
take their parents for granted. Assume they were never
young themselves—but were born old. Never think of
them as having needs, too; of crying in the night. Of
worrying about whether or not they were making the
right parental decisions. Most of all: their being in love
with someone. And here was her mother, still passionately in love with someone whose memory was already
dimming to his children. *So that's what love is all about,*
mused the girl. *Isn't that what Thomas Moore's song is all*
about? She resumed reading:

You've been kinder to me than I deserve. You always
have been one of the most sensitive, empathetic, and
thoughtful persons I've ever known. And forgiving. You
played the game even when you didn't want to continue
it—I know it has been increasingly hard to keep it up in
recent weeks. I can see it in your eyes and body language.
Now it's time for your mother to back off and leave the
big question and decision up to you and John. I suspect it
will be soon. I'm also releasing John from his promise to

me. Yes, *wretched woman that I am, I did sink to collusion. I hope you will someday forgive me for it.*

*Most of all, I hope you will be as happy as your father
and I—*

[and here there was a blot on the inked words that
followed]

> *All my love,*
> *Mom*

Never before had Charity been assailed by such a
tempest of tears. When she finally got out of her chair
and reached for her handkerchief, the child was left
behind, and it was a woman who stood there with
unseeing eyes, staring out into the foggy morning.

✳ ✳ ✳

It was Christmas Eve—and all the gifts had been passed
out but two. With a heart thudding like a great bass
drum, Charity pulled the drapes aside and lifted out
something very large, something that appeared to be a
picture on an easel. Faith helped her carry it out and
place it in front of an astonished John. Charity then
pulled off the wrapper.

Everyone gasped. Here was a man—a young man
who looked familiar yet also larger and grander than life,
standing under a mist-dampened willow one early
morning. Through the leaves could be seen the river,
sorrel but streaked with silver. The man was thrumming
a guitar and looking up with an expression so clearly

portrayed that the first impression on the viewer was to turn away: this was too private for outside eyes to see! John studied it the longest, then looked at Charity with awe. "You painted *that?*"

Charity nodded.

"This is a masterpiece of reflected light! Where did you learn to paint like this?"

"Oh, I had good teachers. And Mom and Dad took us to all the great galleries. For some unknown reason, ever since I was a child, I've been drawn to painters who attempted to capture character expression as revealed by reflected light, such as from an unseen fire-place."

"Which painters?"

"Oh, let's see. . . . Zurbarán in Spain. One of his paintings I stared at for several hours! Rembrandt in Holland. De la Tour in France—what a master of light he was! Caravaggio in Italy. I've always envied his ability to capture flesh tones. And Harry Anderson in America. He painted a lot of covers for popular magazines the first half of the twentieth century."

By this time all the family was gathered around them and the painting, almost overpowered by it and the promise it gave of other such masterpieces to follow. John sank to one knee, took Charity's slim hand in his, and reverently kissed it, saying, "I've met a master! I'm—I'm almost afraid of her."

❊ ❊ ❊

Charity's present from John was a simple ivory envelope with her name on it and these further words: "Please do not open until you are alone." Consequently it was much later before she shut her bedroom door, walked over to her bed, leaned back against the pillows, and opened it. It was very short, and there was no enclosure, yet Charity sensed it was bigger than it looked:

> *My very dear Charity,*
>
> *This will be our second Christmas together.*
>
> *I have a Christmas present for you, but somehow I want to give it to you when we are alone together. As you know, such moments have been rare.*
>
> *I've asked Mother Mary to excuse us for a while tomorrow morning. Told her we'd be back in time for Christmas brunch and that I have a very special Christmas present for you. She knows what it is, and it has her blessing.*
>
> *So I hope you don't feel it's presumptuous of me to abduct you for a few hours. We'll be chaperoned by Sam and Dan.*
>
> *More snow is expected tonight, so I'll have the sleigh at the front gate by 8:00 tomorrow morning. Unless I hear to the contrary from you tonight, I'll expect to see you then. I can hardly wait!*
>
> *Sweet dreams, my dear!*
>
> *Love,*
>
> *John*

What could it possibly be? Whatever it was, though, she sensed some sort of a showdown in the offing: that a question would be asked and an answer expected. An answer that would profoundly impact the rest of their lives.

That her mother both knew of it and approved was a huge relief. To sneak away with John on Christmas morning without such a blessing would be unthinkable. Undoubtedly, Mother had known about this when she wrote that tearstained letter the first week of the Christmas season. This made the event even more significant.

Charity smiled as thoughts of John flooded in on her. He was *so* dear. She, too, could hardly wait!

※ ※ ※

At quarter to eight Christmas morning, while it was still dark, John left the barn with Dan and Sam pulling the sleigh. Thanks to the outside gas torches, Mother Mary was able to watch from the kitchen window, and Faith and Hope from their respective bedroom windows, as the sleigh bells rang and the already snow-coated Belgians snorted and cut up as they came up the long driveway to the house. Just as the team began to slow, a starry-eyed young woman in black and scarlet coat and ski cap slipped out of the house, waved to three windows, and climbed aboard the sleigh. In only moments, they'd been swallowed up by the predawn darkness and the falling snow.

Heavy blankets and mittens kept them warm. Had the horses not known the way so well, John would have lost the trail, so he wisely let them take the lead. Both man and woman were surprisingly tongue-tied, but it was a good silence, for he had the morning scripted according to plan, and she had complete trust in him.

As they looked ahead at the horses, and covertly at each other in the falling snow, their thoughts raced like

Niagara in springtime thaw though words did not come. Subconsciously, each sensed that nothing in their lives before, and nothing after, would ever compare to this heart-stopping morning. Inwardly, each was ever so grateful to Mother Mary for making this morning possible, not just by giving permission for them to share it alone—but far more significantly, by her wise counsel. Because of it, they'd had time to fall in love with the other's soul, to become soul mates. It was enough that Charity's hand was tucked in John's arm and her head occasionally rested on his shoulder.

Half an hour later, clearing skies made possible another gift: Just as dawn broke, in the distance loomed a building she'd never seen—a white-coated log cabin on a hill overlooking frozen-over Half Moon Lake. Smoke spiraled up out of the chimney. Her lips contoured in an *O,* and her hands flew to her cheeks in joy. Turning to John, she sang out, "So *this* is what you've been doing up here all these months!"

John just smiled. As they drew closer, the morning sun gilded both the cabin windows and the icy lake below. Once they reached it, John quickly tethered the Belgians. Then he took Charity's hand and led her up the steps into the cabin.

Inside a fire roared in the massive rock fireplace, which was flanked by bookcases begging for books to fill them. Kerosene lamps gave the big room a homey feel. On the wooden floor was a large blanket rug in a Chief Joseph design, graced by two wooden rockers.

Looking up at the high ceiling and the great logs, she said, "John, you couldn't have done all this by yourself!"

"You're right there. Had an old-fashioned house-raising. Neighbors rode over and helped me (with hoists) to raise these logs and lower them into their slots. Another neighbor came over later and helped me with the three fireplaces."

"Three?"

"Let me show you. First is the basement one—watch your step! As you can see, other than the fireplace and floor it's still unfinished." She silently took in the warm fire crackling in the rock fireplace, the bookcases, and the kerosene lamps positioned on small shelves protruding from the log walls.

"Now, let's go back upstairs, dear. There's more to see. . . . Keep going; there's another floor. . . . Here it is, the master bedroom."

"My, it's almost finished!"

It was indeed. She walked over to the fireplace and warmed her hands over the flames. On the wooden floor were hand-hooked rugs and, on one of them, a large, comfortable looking sofa. Her wondering eyes took it all in: bookcases, a bathroom, a deep closet, windows across one entire side of the room. And glass doors.

"Where do those doors go?" she asked.

"Why don't you find out?"

"Why, a veranda overlooking the lake! What a view!"

❄ ❄ ❄

She'd seen everything, even to the kitchen/dining room which she declared "a dream." Clearly puzzled, though, she wrinkled up her forehead and asked another ques-

tion: "John, where did all these windows and furnishings come from?"

"Wondered when you'd ask that question. It wasn't
that difficult. As you know, because of all the families
that died out during the Dark Time, there are
hundreds of empty houses in the province. A lot of
the fixtures and furnishings have been destroyed—but
a lot remain. Dan and Sam helped me find what was
left, and we hauled the items I liked best up to the
cabin. Where there was an owner, we bartered a fair
price."

Her face softened. "John, who built these fires and lit
them?"

"Me."

"Who filled the lamps and lit them?"

"Me."

"Why?"

He looked into her eyes and said, "You mean, you
really don't know?"

Those lips he'd yet to kiss curved adorably as she
answered, "Of course I have my suspicions—but a
woman likes to hear the *words.*"

John, instead of answering in words, pulled a set of
plans out of a wide drawer, unrolled them, and called
her over. "As you can see, dear, the cabin is still small.
And, even so, a number of rooms are still unfinished. If
you'll follow my pencil, you'll see the rooms that can be
added on later. See?"

"Yes, I see," she answered impishly, "but who's
going to live in them?"

After a long pause, he said, "I've been trying to get to
that."

"But aren't you just a tad slow at getting there?"

How he laughed! Then he said, "Perhaps so. It's just that for fourteen months, I've been living with a dream—trying to make it real."

"Oh?"

"Well, dear, do you remember that dream home you told me about last year?"

She turned to look out the window. "You mean, that day by the lake?"

"Yes. . . . Well, is this it?"

"It is! It *is!* I *love* it! It's everything I dreamed it might be."

"Thank the good Lord!"

Like quicksilver, her expression changed from one of joy to one more than a little shaded with exasperation: "John, don't you think you're putting the cart before the horse"

This time, he got the message. Taking her into his arms, he said, "Will you marry me?"

"Yes, dearest." And in her eyes was everything he had ever longed for. The long game over at last, he collected his winnings.

He kissed her.

❋ ❋ ❋

"John, it's almost time for brunch back home. But before we get back into the sleigh, I have something to say to you. Had you rushed this courtship, I . . . uh . . . don't know that I could have said it. But you've been so adorably shy, that I'm going to. . . . Remember that morning by the river?"

"How could I forget it!"

"Well, you sang words that touched my heart. I knew then, for *sure*, that I loved you enough to spend the rest of my life with you. But where love is concerned, my paintbrush is more articulate than my words—so I've had to go 'a-borrowing.' I searched a long time before I found *just* the right words written by another deeply-in-love woman a long time ago. As I speak these words, please forget that other woman—because, because . . ." and her face flamed. "Oh, John, it's because I love you so! . . . No, stay where you are—or I'll never get through!"

How do I love thee? Let me count the ways.
I love thee to the depth and breadth and height
My soul can reach, when feeling out of sight
For the ends of Being and ideal Grace.
I love thee to the level of everyday's
Most quiet need, by sun and candle-light.
I love thee freely, as men strive for Right;
I love thee purely, as they turn from Praise.
I love thee with the passion put to use
In my old griefs, and with my childhood's faith.
I love thee with a love I seemed to lose
With my lost saints—I love thee with the breath,
Smiles, tears, of all my life!—and, if God choose,
I shall but love thee better after death.

— *"How Do I Love Thee," from Elizabeth Barrett Browning's* Sonnets from the Portuguese

HOW THIS STORY CAME TO BE

First of all, it almost didn't. I had only two weeks in which to write it before a trip to Spain, Gibraltar, Morocco, and Portugal. So I wrote one of my shorter Christmas stories. After completing it, I sent it off to my four faithful story readers and left for Europe. When I returned, to my dismay (but not to my surprise), they told me I would fail my readers if I didn't heave it out the window and write another.

So . . . , back to square one. Again, I prayed that the Lord would give me a story. Only this time, I promised to do justice to whatever plot He gave me, whatever time or effort it took to do it.

Fresh in my mind was the World Trade Center tragedy, as was the worldwide slowdown in the economy that followed.

I was also impressed to stir in part of a letter the western author Louis L'Amour wrote me in connection with my doctoral research on Zane Grey and the Old West, on January 27, 1975. I had asked L'Amour whether or not he agreed with Grey's portrayal of the Old West. Instead of answering directly, in a long three-page letter L'Amour told me what *he* felt the Old West had been. Included were these retrospective and prophetic observations:

> *There is this very important point, often overlooked: a place and a time demand the virtues essential to that place and time.*
>
> *Man's moral codes are a direct development of necessity, and when the necessity is not great, they grow lax and open.*

> *Few women in the west [Old West]—they were*
> *respected, a good woman valued highly, never treated*
> *with disrespect unless by some drunk who might be*
> *quickly hung for it.*
>
> *Married young because of the need for protection, a*
> *home, and to maintain the stock. And because it was the*
> *custom elsewhere. Also because many parents felt that if a*
> *girl were married she was "safe."*
>
> *A startling change in our world would alter our moral*
> *standards overnight.*
>
> *Suppose, for example, a sudden ice-age? A collapse of*
> *our mechanical, industrial world so we'd be back to a*
> *pioneering life?*
>
> *Women's lib would be the first casualty; the home*
> *would become all important; men would revert to weap-*
> *ons to protect their homes and what little they had. . . .*

That quotation from L'Amour has haunted me for
twenty-eight years now, and it came back to me as I
pondered the plot for this story. Especially his line about
a "sudden ice-age" or "collapse of our mechanical,
industrial world so we'd be back to a pioneering life."
Terrorism could easily be responsible for the latter, but
what about the sudden ice-age? What if it were only a
short one?

And that brought me to Krakatoa, one single small
volcano in what is now Indonesia. It was only 2,623 feet
high when it erupted in May 1883. But it was August
before the big blow came. The volcano dropped a thousand feet under the sea, then it virtually exploded. Islands
disappeared forever; new islands suddenly appeared. Thou-
sand-foot waterfalls suddenly appeared in the open sea,

over which went ships to their doom. More people died from Krakatoa than in the Lisbon earthquake of 1755. The sky was pitch-black as far away as 150 miles. Dust and ashes shot up more than seventeen miles into the atmosphere. The sound was heard three thousand miles away, and fifty-foot-high tidal waves swept forward and backwards across the oceans of the world, one smashing into Cape Horn (7,818 miles away). Eventually the seething mass of materials belched out of the earth's mantle permeated the clouds and spread across North and South America, Europe, Asia, Africa, and Australia. It changed the climate of the entire world for several years; in some areas, the effect was characterized as "the year with no summer." And I couldn't help but wonder, *If one volcano could do this much damage, change the climate to this extent, just think of the impact of multiple volcanic eruptions over a sequence of years! Might they not cause a sudden, but perhaps short, ice-age?*

Where geology is concerned, I was way beyond my depths, so I consulted Monte Swan, a professor of chemistry and geology. He suggested that I rewrite my entire preamble, which I dutifully did.

And I thought about the phenomenon of homeschooling that is currently sweeping across the nation. The three protagonists of the story, Faith, Hope, and Charity, I saw at a large homeschooling conference in Grand Rapids, Michigan, last January (a large number of girls and young women just like my three heroines). I faithfully attempted to transplant them to Canada in my story, in all their multidimensionality.

Sam and Dan (under different names) actually pulled a sleigh my wife and I rode in near Keystone, Colorado, about a year ago. The driver told us about the characteristics of the breed (their teaming for life—even to the nipping and pooping on the harness!).

Sheree Parris Nudd of Maryland enlightened me on homing pigeons, Evan Nudd on gas well distribution, and Linda Steinke of Alberta filled me in on Canadian life (helping me with verisimilitude).

And, as a historian of ideas, I am well aware that every *fin de siècle* brings with it seismic societal changes. Five-hundred-year turns are even more explosive: The one a thousand years ago spawned the Crusades and the great Age of Faith during which Europe's soaring Gothic cathedrals were built. The one five centuries later was preceded by the Renaissance and followed by the Reformation.

So, I've wondered, *what happens now, as we've just experienced the century and millennial turns four years ago?* Huge changes will inevitably occur; we just don't know which ones. All we know is that the nation and world will be far different from what they were before the year 2000. They already are.

Putting it all together, the Lord gave me the plot: the Dark Time and its aftermath, a Voice in the night, and a young man starting out on foot, going north. From that point on, I stumbled all over the place for I kept assuming certain things were probable that, in light of the complete breakdown of society, most definitely were not. I had to come up with new assumptions (both inclusions and exclusions). This resulted in my having to rewrite a large part of the story. As to the Westcott household, that caught me by surprise as well. I had John continuing north; the Lord had him staying there with the Westcotts. You've seen who won out.

FOCUS ON THE FAMILY®
Welcome to the Family!

It began in 1977 with the vision
of Dr. James Dobson, a licensed psychologist
and author of best-selling books on marriage,
parenting, and family. Alarmed by the many
pressures threatening the American family,
he founded Focus on the Family, now an
international organization dedicated
to preserving family values through the
life-changing message of Jesus Christ.

• • •

For more information about the ministry,
or if we can be of help to your family, simply
write to Focus on the Family, Colorado
Springs, CO 80995 or call 1-800-A-FAMILY
(1-800-232-6459). Friends in Canada may write
Focus on the Family, P.O. Box 9800, Stn. Terminal,
Vancouver, B.C. V6B 4G3, or call 1-800-661-9800.
Visit our Web site at www.family.org
(in Canada, www. focusonthefamily.ca).

We'd love to hear from you!

Joe Wheeler fan? Like curling up with a good story? Try these other Joe Wheeler books that will give you that "warm all over" feeling.

HEART TO HEART STORIES OF LOVE

Remember old-fashioned romance? The hauntingly beautiful, gradual unfolding of the petals of love, leading up to the ultimate full flowering of marriage and a lifetime together? From the story of the young army lieutenant returning from World War II to meet his female pen pal at Grand Central Station in the hope that their friendship will develop into romance, to the tale of a young woman who finds love in the romantic history of her grandmother, this collection satisfies the longing for stories of genuine, beautiful, lasting love.

Heart to Heart Stories of Love will warm your heart with young love, rekindled flames, and promises kept.
0-8423-1833-X

HEART TO HEART STORIES OF FRIENDSHIP

A touching collection of timeless tales that will uplift your soul. For anyone who has ever experienced or longed for the true joy of friendship, these engaging stories are sure to inspire laughter, tears, and tender remembrances. Share them with a friend or loved one.
0-8423-0586-6

HEART TO HEART STORIES FOR DADS

This collection of classic tales is sure to tug at your heart and take up permanent residence in your memories. These stories about fathers, beloved teachers, mentors, pastors, and other father figures are suitable for reading aloud to the family or for enjoying alone for a cozy evening's entertainment.
0-8423-3634-6

HEART TO HEART STORIES FOR MOMS

This heartwarming collection includes stories about the selfless love of mothers, stepmothers, surrogate mothers, and mentors. Moms in all stages of life will cherish stories that parallel their own, those demonstrating the bond between child, mother, and grandmother. A collection to cherish for years to come.
0-8423-3603-6

HEART TO HEART STORIES FOR SISTERS

Heart to Heart Stories for Sisters is a touching collection of classic short stories that is sure to become a family favorite. These stories about sisters and the relationships that bind them together are perfect for reading aloud to the whole family, for giving to your own sister, or simply for enjoying alone.
0-8423-5378-X

HEART TO HEART STORIES FOR GRANDPARENTS

Grandparents and grandchildren share a special bond—because there's something almost magical about that relationship. From the story of a man who lovingly cares for his grandmother after she develops Alzheimer's disease, to the tale of a woman whose advice helps her great-granddaughter decide which man to marry, this beautiful volume will touch your heart and encourage you to savor the time you spend with family members—of all generations.
0-8423-5379-8

HEART TO HEART STORIES FOR TEACHERS

Good teachers open up the world for their students—and leave a permanent legacy in the hearts and minds of those whose lives they touch. This moving collection of stories portrays the inspiring relatinships between teachers and their students, from the one-room schoolhouse to the college classroom. Perfect for reading alone or sharing with a favorite teacher.
0-8423-5412-3

CHRISTMAS IN MY HEART
Volume IX

From the tale of the orphan boy who loses a beloved puppy but finds a loving home for Christmas, to the narrative of an entire town that gives an impoverished family an unexpectedly joyful Christmas, these heartwarming stories will touch your soul with the true spirit of the season. Featured authors include O. Henry, Grace Livingston Hill, Margaret Sangster, Jr., and others.

Christmas is a time for families to take time to sit together, perhaps around a crackling blaze in the fireplace, and reminisce about Christmases of the past. Enjoy the classic stories found in this book and understand why thousands of families have made the Christmas in My Heart series part of their traditions.
0-8423-5189-2

CHRISTMAS IN MY HEART
Volume X

Christmas in My Heart, Volume 10 will bring a tear to your eye and warmth to your heart as you read the story of a lonely little girl who helps a heartbroken mother learn to love again, or the tale of a cynical old shopkeeper who discovers the true meaning of Christmas through the gift of a crippled man. Authors include Pearl S. Buck, Harry Kroll, Margaret Sangster, Jr., and others.
0-8423-5380-1

CHRISTMAS IN MY HEART
Volume XI

The Christmas season is a time for reflection and peace, a time with family and friends. As you read the story of a father desperately searching for the perfect gift for his little girl, or the account of two brothers who learn a meaningful lesson about God's love from a pair of scrawny Christmas trees, you'll expereience anew the joys and meaning of the season.
0-8423-5626-6

CHRISTMAS IN MY HEART
Volume XII

Open *Christmas in My Heart, Volume 12* and find hope and joy in the collection of stories gathered. A variety of fifteen heartwarming stories—from Arizona senator John McCain's most memorable Christmas among his fellow POWs in a North Vietnamese prison cell, to a warm haven from a Christmas Eve blizzard, to an aged shepherd's eyewitness account of a miracle in Bethlehem— each selection reminds the reader of the true meaning of Christmas.
0-8423-7126-5